ACKNOWLEDGEMENTS

To the cold Christmas days that
kept me hidden under the covers
with the warm body of another.

... And to the heated nights
that required no fireplace
because there was heat enough
under the covers from friction.

How Santa Ate My Cookies

... And other Festive Tales of Erotic Fiction

BY

TITUS STRONG

wunderlannd WP press

How Santa Ate My Cookies
…and Other Festive Tales of Erotic Fiction

Published by Wunderlannd Press Publishing, LLC
Murfreesboro, Tennessee

"We plunged into the cornucopia quivering with desire and the ecstasy of unbridled avarice."

- Ralphie, from the film *A Christmas Story*

FOREWORD

Holy smokes! It's about that time! Yes, indeed. This book has been 'long in coming' (heh, heh). I think that everyone, especially during the holiday season, deserves a break... of the naughty kind. When most people think about X-mas, it's always this simple list: presents, tree, X-mas carols, eggnog, and vacation time with a little bit of snow flurries. But for me, it's a little bit different.

For me, well...

I like the idea of being on Santa's naughty list. All of the best holiday films had those on the naughty list. Hell, everyone loves the villain! Some of the most iconic characters in film are villains. So, why not root for those that are naughty/bad in an erotic fiction?

Well, I'm here today to advocate for the naughty ones out there.

For some reason, (I don't know why really), I like to talk about my virgin moments. This is the first time for me... writing a published series of short stories. I feel it fitting that they be covered in the smut and grime of ages gone and some still yet to come. It is fitting because, with all the stories that I have inside of my head, these are the ones that I can let go completely with, allowing the stories to present themselves to you without reluctance.

With what I write for a more serious crowd, plot, story, characters, as well as resolutions are involved as long as it's connected with a long-running storyline. But these are a bit different. For these tales, as you open the pages and read each depraved, selfless and extremely gratifying short story, see for yourself. There are no expectations that await you here; only what you bring with you.

These will entertain you without a doubt. There is no question there. Each story is likely to catch fire within your mind and run down through your veins to your naughty parts and have them begging for release!

So, without further ado, drop trou and get the lube.

Enjoy yourself as only you see fit!

Titus Strong

Smoking a cigarette after being

in a compromising position

September 9, 2011

Christmas Break with a Twist

Written by Titus Strong

CHAPTER ONE
- "I'M DREAMING..." -

"Are you ready for this?"

A satisfactory number of women had answered this question with a resounding yes throughout Austin Tagger's college years, many a time with panties around their ankles and a sly grin plastered on their face with the idea that something naughty was about to happen; which, of course, naughty usually did occur when Austin was in the picture. But the look on Karen's face was different.

Moreover, her panties weren't around her ankles and she didn't give a resounding yes. As both of them packed up their bags in the back of Karen's 98 Chrysler Lebaron, Austin could literally cut the tension with a knife.

On the phone she sounded fine, he reminded himself, packing his smaller bag in with the rest of the bags as well as wrapped presents for her family in the trunk, Austin shutting it shortly after.

"Is something wrong, Karen?"

Karen forced a smile and shook her head without speaking, *a definite sign that something was up*, Austin concluded, getting into the passenger's seat of the white Lebaron. Karen pushed the glasses up onto her nose the rest of the way, the round frames hiding well what she thought and felt behind the glare of the panel lighting of her car. It was already past midnight and they were getting started late. But, of course, Austin couldn't help himself with Karen.

If I know how it is at family homes, we won't have a moment of privacy and we won't be able to have sex again until we get back.

If anything, that 45-minute session on her roommate's freshly made bed did him some good. Sure, he was left a little tired and sleepy-eyed from the grunt-inducing orgasm he had left on the clean bed sheets, but he was taken care of until they got back....he hoped.

Ten days! A full week and a half of nothing but a family that I haven't met yet that have Karen's genes!

Austin looked at the shy, mousy girl that he had ended up with too close to the holidays to let go of. It was a rule for him that anyone he kept before or after Thanksgiving would remain until after the New Year, which meant that he would have to stay around even if he didn't want to. After all, he didn't want to be without something warm and wet for the New Year. It was too late to find someone else and he knew that, especially after finding out his parents were on a cruise holiday and wouldn't be celebrating Christmas this year, he didn't have anywhere else to go.

Austin had seen Karen's gaze on him a number of times throughout the semester. Of course, it wasn't uncommon to see the stares, especially from the younger freshman and sophomores that the college ushered in every semester.

Everyone knew about Austin Tagger. Deemed Tagger the "Tagger" because of his prowess at "tagging" the offensive line that came near him on the football field, his teammates in the locker room took it another way as well. Soon, Tagger the "Tag-her" had been invented. After hearing some of Austin's sexual escapades with a few of the cheerleaders as well as some of the student council, his teammates kept the nickname in check and continually on their tongues throughout football season.

But Karen was different than the other girls he messed around with. Karen was Austin's little secret away from everyone else in college. As the last game of the holiday season wrapped, Austin had much more time on his hands to hang out at the college media center and bait Karen for the holidays. It was a library, sure, but it came with a number of delights for one of the hunkiest college football seniors, who could get his veritable pick of the litter of some of the finer college girls.

But there was something, a secret of sorts that was kept in the darker, less-used places inside everyone's soul, and his place called out for Karen and Karen only. Maybe it was all the times that Austin had gone out and hung out with brainless, walking vaginas that had done him in. But he actually liked Karen. She was normal. She was the Janet in *Three's Company*, the Mary Ann in *Gilligan's Island*. She was the safe girl. But, deep down inside Austin's mind, he hoped that she was a fiery vixen under the covers.

At the present, she had been a bit submissive with sex, allowing him to have his way with her somewhat easily, which didn't really turn him on in the least. He was sure there would be another warm body filling his nights shortly after New Years Eve.

The drive from Murfreesboro, Tennessee to Frankfort, Kentucky, where Karen's family lived, was slated at four hours. They still had to fuel up and get something to eat as well as get any snacks that they would need along the way. It was December 23rd and all was well just on the outskirts of the MTSU college campus, many of the college kids having already left for the holidays. The two of them stopped at the IHOP just off Old Fort Parkway before starting on the interstate and made their way in.

After being seated, they ordered a late breakfast and started on their coffee. Austin thought that this was the best time as any and tried for some conversation.

"Alright, Karen. I know something is wrong. I can't read minds but I can feel it coming off of you!"

Karen just straightened her posture a bit more and huddled into her winter coat, the scarf covering from her neck up to her ears.

"What are you talking about, Austin?" She was the best at playing coy.

"This vibe! I don't know. I feel something. If we have such a long drive ahead of us, I would at least like it to be friendly."

The waitress came by and assured them that their meals would be on the way shortly and Karen affirmed that something was indeed wrong to him. She didn't say anything, but her eyes told it. Austin knew that they had only known one another for a few short months, just since October, but they had spent a little quality time together since then. Then she said it.

"I like you, Austin. I really do. I have since I came to MTSU as a freshman. You're attractive, you're smart for a jock, and you've finally given me the time of day with you, which means that I get a chance to show you why I'm different than all the other girls."

"I know you're different, Karen."

"Yes, but not in a positive way. You and many like you see me as an outcast. I'm an outcast for a reason, Austin. I choose to be."

Austin just shook his head.

"Why would you choose to be an outcast? That's no fun."

Karen just smiled at him and leaned back a little in the booth as the waitress brought their food, sitting it out before them on the table. She didn't answer right away. Karen took delight in the fact that something as simple as herself perplexed Austin Tagger, the great and powerful football player. In fact, this had been her plan all along.

It wasn't until they were on the road, had gotten fuel and snacks and were well on their way on Interstate 65 going north that Karen spoke again about it. Austin had let the topic go when Karen had not spoken of it again but, as they passed the Tennessee-Kentucky border entering into Kentucky, Karen finally decided to bring it up.

"Promise me that you won't say anything about our time up here with my family to anyone you know."

"Why?"

Karen's face was barely visible in the low light of the car when she answered back.

"I mean, you can tell people that you came to visit with my family for Christmas, but I've told everyone that you had no one to spend it with because your family was on a cruise and you were without a place to stay, which is not completely a lie."

Austin did his best to figure Karen out, but his brain wasn't working at the moment. He didn't know if it was the sex or the pancakes, but he had a major case of the lazies.

"Alright. So, you have a weird family, I understand. Everyone is scared for other people to meet their family. Hell, hardly anyone I know from college has met my family!"

"No, I mean what happens between us!"

"Oh, okay. Well, what do you have planned for us?" Austin looked over at her with a sly grin. Even though he was satiated for the moment, he would always be willing to have a quickie pulled over on the side of the road. But, then again, Karen wasn't really that type of girl. He had trouble picturing her taking control in any part of her life, especially when it came to sex.

"It's not what I have planned, Austin, it's what happens during Christmas that I can't control." She didn't look at him when she said that, instead focusing on the dark roads ahead of them as they cast shadows as the car pushed onward.

Immediately, Austin's mind drifted off to a long list of cheesy horror movies: *Wrong Turn, Cabin Fever, High Tension, Hostel,* as well as a great many others that he had watched with his friends a couple of years back. They all left a lasting impression upon his psyche to never leave his comfort zone and, as he looked out in front of him at the road that passed underneath them, he knew he had left his comfort zone somewhere back in Tennessee.

"Can't control? What are you talking about? You're starting to freak me out a little, Karen!"

But then came Karen's comforting smile, the small dimples on the sides of her face appearing. She giggled a bit and that eased Austin's stress inside of his mind momentarily.

"No, silly! Not like that! My family are not a bunch of freaks and neither am I! You're crazy, Austin! That's why I like you so much. I'm just a different person when I'm away from college. Especially around the holidays."

"Well, as long as you're not a serial killer, I think I can handle anything you throw at me. After all, I am a jock, right?"

He then felt Karen's invisible hand reach down in between his legs in the dark and squeeze the outline of his cock between her fingers through his jeans.

"Yes, you are!"

Oh my god, this girl is a freak! This is exactly what I hoped for! Thank you, Santa Claus! My Christmas wish was coming true.

However, Austin Tagger had no idea what kind of naughty list Karen Meyers was on but was soon about to find out.

It wasn't long before they rolled into Frankfort, Kentucky and were only miles away from her parent's house. Here came the disclaimer that Austin had been waiting for.

"Just to let you know, Austin, I've never brought anyone home to meet my family. They aren't weird or anything, but they really celebrate Christmas, in a kooky kind of way."

"I'm down with that. Are there any rules that I need to go by?"

"Well, you'll be my boyfriend going in, if you don't mind. And I don't really know how they will take to that. I've had boyfriends in high school and my freshman year in college, but I never really told them about them. My personal life is sort of personal to me. I don't let my family in too much with that."

"Okay. I'm your boyfriend." Austin had to repeat it several times in his head so that he was comfortable with it. Then he continued.

"What else?"

Karen stopped the car in an abandoned parking area for this. She put the car in park and looked over at the football player.

"I know who you are and what type of guy you are, Austin! Don't think that I'm naïve or a lost, little girl!"

Austin was almost offended but knew exactly what she was talking about. He hadn't hidden his agenda for any woman. Whenever a woman got with Austin, they knew what they were in store for. There was no permanence there; nothing that stood for anything more than a good time. So, with knowing that, Austin considered that Karen was another just like the others when she accepted his invitation to a night out with a popular, good-looking football player.

And Karen just confirmed it.

"Why do you think I would think that?" Austin tried his best to play dumb but Karen was too smart for that.

"Let's cut through the red tape of this situation, shall we? You're here for play and nothing serious. I want you to know that I know that and I'm okay with that. I want the same thing. But, when we go into my parent's house, I would like for them not to see that. I don't want them thinking that I'm just going to get hurt by you or I'm being used by you in some way. Can we just go in as a couple and pretend to be in love or something like that? Just for a few days?"

Austin was dumbfounded. It was so straightforward, so cut and dry. Sure, he had played this part a number of times in different scenarios over the years, but to have it laid out so formally was something that made his head spin. He couldn't help but say yes.

I mean, it sounded harmless enough, right?

"So, you want me to pretend for the holidays that we're head over heels for one another in front of your family?"

"Yes."

"And we both go back to college afterward and everything returns to normal and no one has to know anything happened?"

"Exactly." The mousy little Karen behind the glasses waited for Austin to respond.

This was getting better and better by the moment, Austin agreed, turning back comfortably in his seat as Karen shifted the car into drive and moved out of the parking area, veering onto a small highway road, only a few miles away from her parent's home.

"I think I can do that."

CHAPTER TWO
" …OF A WHITE… "

And do that, Austin Tagger did. It wasn't long before they were unpacking their things at her parent's home; Laura and Skip were the nicest folks, with Karen taking on aspects of both of her parent's features easily. She was short and slender like her mother, who helpfully showed Austin around the two-story colonial, letting Austin take the empty bedroom next to Karen's room.

"My, you're quite a big boy, aren't you?" Austin stood almost a foot taller than Karen's mom, who barely broke 5-foot 6 inches in height, the same wavy brown hair that her daughter had. To Austin, she looked like an aged Lisa Loeb, from Lisa Loeb and the Nine Stories, a band his older sister had listened to.

If Karen's mom only knew how big I was. And how I filled her daughter up just a few hours ago.

But none of his depraved thoughts managed to slip out of his mouth. If anything, Austin played the well-mannered young man to the tee, complete with the yes ma'ams and no ma'ams of generations past. His parents and grandparents had taught him quite well and manners weren't a thing of the past for him. Just because he was banging this woman's daughter in the privacy of a series of random places, it gave him no reason to be disrespectful.

"Yes, ma'am. They grow 'em big in Tennessee."

"Well, they sure do! This is Karen's older brother's room, David. He's away in the military right now, serving our country, so I'm sure he won't mind if you make use of it while you're here. The main washroom is the second door on the left and there are washcloths and towels in the linen closet just behind the door once you enter."

"Thank you, Mrs. Meyers."

Karen's mother blushed and patted him playfully on the arm.

"Oh, please, call me Laura! You're a guest while you're here, not a stranger." She began to leave and turned back around.

"Austin, now I'm going to leave you to get unpacked and comfortable. I know it's been a long drive, so I'm going to leave you for the evening. So, if there's anything you need, Skip and I are in the room all the way at the end of the hallway. But I'm sure my little girl will take good care of you! She was always such a good hostess!"

And, with that said, Austin was alone with his bags and the lingering smell of apple and cinnamon that came from the Glade plug-in not far from the bed.

It was Christmastime indeed at the Meyer's family home tonight!

The next morning, Austin woke up fairly early. It wasn't the strange bed, which slept rather well he noticed, or being in a strange place for the first time; he had grown accustomed to traveling to different places throughout his college football experience, especially just for a night or two. It was the smell of food. Somehow, it overpowered the Glade plug-in and made his olfactory senses awaken in protest that he had not eaten anything else the night before. After all, he had not snacked on any of the items that they had bought at the gas station after eating that late breakfast.

The football player made his way downstairs, fully knowing that his appetite, especially with his bulk intake and work out plan that had kept him in full, physical form for the season would take over, especially since it was the Christmas season.

"Good morning, Austin! Hope you slept well." Karen's father Skip was up and already dressed in a shirt and tie. He sported a matching briefcase and seemed to be in a hurry as he buzzed past the younger man, a cup of coffee in hand. They had met for moments last night and it seemed that it would be the same this morning.

"I'm sorry, Austin. I have to work this morning; damn company called me in! I'll try to get back before it gets too late and you guys have all the fun! Sound good?"

Still half-asleep, Austin nodded kindly and watched as Karen's father moved out of the kitchen and was gone in a flash. Austin heard a noise by the sink and noticed that Karen's mother was up already as well, her morning robe on over her nightclothes. She divvied out some eggs from a skillet onto three plates at the breakfast counter.

"Good morning, Austin. Karen said she'd be down in a minute. You know young ladies; they always have to freshen up in the morning." Austin knew this all too well. He had slept over many a college girl's dorm room and knew the morning ritual.

"That's fine, Mrs. Meyers, I mean Laura. Sorry. Do you have any more coffee left?"

"Well, I do think we have some coffee left. I'll pour you a cup."

If you can guess, this is how the morning went; most of how mornings go in strange places where you know the normal shit happens on a rigid schedule. But it wasn't until Karen's mom Laura went out for some groceries and ran some other errands that Austin knew he had reached uncharted territory.

It wasn't until Karen was handing him the Christmas tinsel they had gotten from an old box in the attic to decorate the tree with that she spoke the magic words.

"I want to fuck you right now, in front of the tree." And there wasn't the "your mother's coming home soon speech" that a male would normally give to let the moment subside and save that lust for later. Austin saw something in Karen's eyes that he had not seen before and decided it was best to not let it disappear. So, in moments, Austin was on his back on the floor, shirt pulled up and jeans down past his knees, using the balled-up tree skirt as a pillow for his head as Karen pressed her naked thighs against him urgently. She was wet; wetter than she had ever been with him. Austin could tell because his cock slid right in without any friction at all.

Soon, they were down to business and a little business was just fine for Austin, who slipped Karen's breasts free from the bra she wore and held them in his palms, letting her keep the pace for the two of them.

For some reason, though, it seemed more urgent than ever before. When Karen came this time, her hands reached out for a stocking in the box near them and stuffed it in her mouth, letting out a moan that reverberated through her torso and shook the very orgasm out of Austin, his hands holding her thighs down against him until his own pleasure erupted deep inside her.

"Fuck, Karen! What the fuck was that?"

But Karen didn't hear him. She pulled the Christmas stocking from her mouth and tossed it back into the box, collapsing on Austin's sweaty and still somewhat heaving chest. Then she whispered in his ear.

"Call me Kitty."

Let us just say that helping unload the groceries from the car to the kitchen was a little awkward for Austin, who was still in the throes of post-coital repose, almost on a high of sorts yet listening still to her mother Laura prattle on about great savings at the local grocery store this holiday season. Somehow, Karen didn't seem fazed by it at all. If anything, she had turned back to her normal, dry self once the garage door could be heard activating, her mother having pulled the car in from the cold, wintry morning. Kitty had pulled herself free from the football player's relaxed grip and slid her jeans back on, still moist and dripping from their encounter, watching as Austin slid his pants back up as well, trying to recover as quick as he could before Karen's mother came in. Karen offered him a hand to help him up.

Soon, both of them were unloading groceries with her mother.

"Oh, I see you got some of the Christmas things out to decorate! Oh, Karen, you're so awful! You know I wanted to do that with you!"

Laura came back in from looking at the living room and finished up putting the remainder of the groceries up and taking the empty plastic bags back into the garage for the recycling bin.

"Oh, mom! You know how I get when it's Christmas!" Karen looked over at Austin, the football player still feeling the wetness from her orgasm pressed against him now that his underwear was on.

"I can't help myself. Christmas just gets me so excited." The comment was more for Austin's pleasure, which worked its way quickly through him, the football player feeling another stirring within him building up.

Laura came back into the room.

"Oh, that's right, Austin! Karen used to get so excited during Christmastime. She used to help me decorate and make cookies and pour hot chocolate. We used to watch all the old Christmas movies at one time. She couldn't get enough of them!" Laura laughed aloud.

"She even convinced me one year to get a small television and VCR to put in her room so she could watch Christmas movies by herself. It was so cute."

But something inside Austin made him think that it wasn't just a cute thing with Karen. As he looked at the timid, shy librarian now, he saw Kitty wanting to come back out and play. Then he remembered taking the box out from the attic and how Karen was nearly out of breath when he did so.

And it wasn't from the hard work. She just stood by the attic stairs. It was if I had unearthed Kitty as well when I brought down the box.   Once they opened the box and started laying the decorations out, that's when her hands were all over him.

And her mouth.

Austin closed his eyes at the thought of it, reliving the sensation down within his pants. He wanted Kitty just as bad as Kitty had wanted him. He was not against it, not in the least, but he had see something that he had never seen before.

This girl gets off on the idea of anything Christmas!

There was something almost animalistic about how Karen had taken control as they were decorating the living room. It was something he hadn't see nearly enough in his time with women while in college. He hoped to see more from Kitty very soon. Laura piped up and broke Austin from his daydreaming state.

"Anybody want cookies?" Laura held out a roll of chocolate chip cookie dough from the fridge, smiling.

And this is how the morning as well as the afternoon proceeded, with very little movement toward the naughty or any remarks from Karen about the dirty little sex that they had on the floor of her parent's living room, almost as if she weren't that person that had rode him hard and left him wet. She kept eye contact with him and talked about college as well as his favorite Christmas memories as a kid as they hung ornaments, soon moving to the mantle to decorate the mantle with reindeer and snowman-shaped mini-statues that lit up, hanging garland through the banisters up the stairs as well.

And there was no more naughty play or talk of naughty play when Karen's father came home from work later that evening, either. In fact, it was your usual night, filled with tales from the office of work and play as well as deals at the grocery from her mother, which Austin still managed to look surprised even though he had heard the story twice already, looking over for signs of Kitty within Karen.

If she was there anywhere, she was hiding herself well, Austin thought to himself.

After dinner, the family and Austin retreated to the living room to watch Christmas movies on television.

CHAPTER THREE
- "...GIRL ON MY COCK!" -

Kitty came to Austin in his dreams later that night. Still thinking about the morning romp with Karen's alternate self, Austin was semi-hard and going to bed by himself in the extra room. Soon, he was sound asleep and dreaming of the continued naughtiness that could occur in the parent's home at any given moment.

It started with Kitty pulling urgently at his covers. Then, once they were down at his ankles, Kitty slipped the boxers off his hips and out from under him, leaving them at his knees, her red velvet Christmas gloves going to work stroking his cock. He couldn't see her face in his dream but he knew she was looking at him; her hard, exact stare cutting into the stillness of the otherwise silent night.

If she doesn't stop soon, the night won't be so silent, Austin thought to himself, his hand moving to his semi-erect cock now, going to work under the covers, the thoughts of Kitty waking him up fully and at the ready, his desire urging himself to come.

I can keep my cock in my boxers and clean up the mess in the morning when I have time in the bathroom, he thought, convincing himself it was a novel idea. *After all, when am I going to get time alone? Or anymore time with Karen? Or Kitty, or whoever she calls herself while we're here.*

Austin did indeed have it planned out well. Nothing got him off to sleep better than a good, stiff orgasm bursting from the tip of his erection out onto his shaking hand. He continued the strokes for a few moments more, thinking again of the naughtiness he had seen in Kitty's eyes earlier today. It all would have worked out fine if Karen hadn't been standing at the edge of his bed, watching his covers jerk up and down haphazardly. It was true, the noise couldn't have been heard from the other rooms, so the first thing that Austin thought about when he saw her there was how she got in without him noticing.

Then he saw the closet door ajar just behind her and knew that she had snuck in while he was in the bathroom brushing his teeth.

She was standing next to him in moments and, though he had stopped his fantasy masturbation, he kept his cock in his hand.

He heard the anger in her voice.

"You're disgusting!" Karen moved closer, nearly eye level with him now. Austin let go of his cock and let it retreat back into the folds of his boxers, nearly shrinking away from shame.

"What?"

"You didn't get enough earlier today that you had to pull out your cock after spending time with my family and start jerking it as soon as you get in here alone?"

"I didn't know you... I thought you..." Austin was stuck between the rock in his pants and a hard place.

"You are a disgusting pig, just like all those girls say at college! You just want to fuck and fuck and fuck all of the time."

"Karen, it's not what you..."

She pressed a gloved finger to his lips.

"I told you to call me Kitty!"

That's when he saw the look in her eyes... and what she wore as she moved closer to him.

Austin was never much for wrapping paper, though what Kitty wore could not be called as such. Slim, tight-fitting red and white lingerie pressed in on her petite frame and made him want to know what hurt her and what felt good to her. Her ample breasts nearly spilled out of the outfit onto Austin's waiting face, his erection perking back up from the cavern of shame.

"Yes, Kitty." Austin was willing to play whatever game she wanted to get himself off. And, if that meant being a naughty boy and feeling ashamed while she rode his cock like a champ, then so be it.

Maybe she likes pain, too! If she likes freaky stuff; if getting fucked at the sight of Christmas garland and a collection of old ornaments gets her off, maybe she likes the rough stuff, too!

"My, you're a naughty boy, aren't you?" Kitty leaned back away from him, Austin reaching out from under the covers to grab for her; but she was already moving back to the closet where she had been hiding.

Lying in wait was more like it, Austin remarked to himself, seeing Kitty return with some multi-colored Christmas tree lights and a medium-sized teddy bear with a red bow tied just under its chin. To Austin, Kitty looked like a model for one of those naughty Christmas calendars you'd buy in Spencer's gift stores or see hanging up at a Hooters restaurant for the holidays.

Yet, this football player didn't mind in the least. In fact, his erection seemed harder than ever underneath the covers. No longer was it ashamed at the idea of being fapped for festive fun. It raised itself high and strong in the name of play and other fore playing festivities.

Already primed and ready to go for some late-night naughty action, Austin smiled when Kitty approached, his hands moving onto her thighs to lead her down and onto his already throbbing member. But she stopped him and took his hands off her hips, leading them up and over Austin's head. Kitty laid the teddy bear down on the bed next to him and straddled him, using the Christmas lights to tie his hands to the bedposts just above him. Austin just smiled the entire time, watching with rapt interest as Kitty's nearly exposed breasts dangled over him, looking ripe and about to burst out of her naughty attire.

Now this is more like it!

"Have I been a naughty boy, Kitty? Are you going to punish me?"

But Kitty just smiled as she finished tying the lights around his wrists; and rather tight, he noticed, noting that he couldn't get free from them, even if he tried.

Kitty's voice was barely a whisper as she grabbed her teddy bear up in her arms and sat on Austin's lap, his stiff cock trapped under the covers still.

"Yes, Austin, you've been naughty....and for that you must be punished."

Austin had no hesitation in his mind about being punished; even being spanked and having some rough play always livened up the rather dull sex that he had been having as of late with the randoms that occupied his dorm room the last few months. But there was something in the way that Kitty said it that left him with some hesitation now that he was tied up and not able do anything to stop her from-

-from what? Chopping me up into little pieces, packing me up in my own luggage and burying me in her back yard?

This and a great many things entered Austin's mind but were quelled just as quickly as he felt the blankets at his waist drop down to his feet at the edge of the bed, Kitty's tongue dragging itself across his chest, to his stomach; her warm tongue hovering just over his boxers, teasing the erection that threatened to break through the flap and assault any and every part of her body that it could.

Well, if that's my punishment, I think I'll be okay!

But it wasn't.

Kitty slipped the boxers off Austin's legs and climbed on top of him, sitting on his lap, teddy bear now in her hands, looking naughty. She leaned forward, pressing her body into his, her free hand flipping a small switch on the lights tied at his wrists. The multi-colored lights lit up and, again, Austin saw the look in Kitty's eyes.

It was that same look that he had seen earlier. As she leaned down against him, the bear was close enough to smell. It smelled of peppermint with a hint of cinnamon and, very lightly, of pine or potpourri, Austin couldn't really tell which.

In another moment, Kitty was back up and sitting on his thighs, the tip of his rigid member pressed against her wet entrance, which he felt dripping down onto his lap in its own anticipation at the festivities to come.

And it was then Austin realized Kitty had no panties on. He could feel the wetness on his leg, pressed against his left thigh. His cock danced its own rendition of the Nutcracker and eagerly awaited something more to happen; but Kitty simply set the stage; for what, Austin had no idea.

The festively clad temptress continued on in her naughty yet nice ways. She allowed her lips to become somewhat pouty and pulled from inside the stuffing of the teddy bear a large candy cane ...except for that it wasn't a candy cane at all. What looked like an oversized peppermint stick was actually a holiday-style vibrator with a handle on it for better handling. As she slid it beneath her naughty outfit, Kitty slid the tip of the candy cane inside her, letting out a soft moan.

"Oh, Austin, you've been a naughty boy!"

Kitty dropped the teddy bear on the floor next to the bed and focused on the vibrating that started between her legs, her thighs tightening up against him as well, her slightly spread legs trying their best to close so the vibrations weren't so strong. Her other hand drifted down between her legs as well, tightening around his cock as she pleasured herself just over him.

Kitty grabbed at the twisted end of the cane and pressed it further into herself, beginning to play with Austin's sizable member at the same time, her fingers as well as part of her palm lightly grazing over the tip and base of his dick, sending pangs of pleasure throughout his limbs as he looked at Kitty's pouty face, now allowing itself to show some pleasure.

"You can't have this, Austin! You had your chance and you were about to blow it all alone. Now all you get to do is watch."

Kitty's extra hand left his cock then and began playing with her nipples, pulling the candy cane vibrator out from her moistness, pressing the tip of it hard against her clit; all the while keeping her eyes locked on Austin's.

She's going to come on me! The football player could see it in her eyes. He knew now what she intended to do; it seemed that was why she had hidden in his room in the first place. In fact, it seemed quite well planned out when he thought about it.

In another few seconds, Austin felt Kitty's knees begin to shake and her eyes closed, raising her face up to the ceiling as the vibrating continued between her legs. But she did not let up. The sex-coated candy cane stayed its course just until the young woman bolted upright, shaking from pleasure, her free hand pressing down on Austin's bare chest to steady herself as the orgasm shot through her.

"Oh fuck, Austin! You could have had this all over your cock! Instead," Kitty gasped, nearly biting her lip as another orgasm escaped from between her legs and against the plastic tip of the vibrating candy cane between her legs, "you only get to watch!" Kitty kept herself upright with her hand, which wavered and almost buckled when the second one took her by surprise.

One thing is for sure; Kitty sure is a trooper!

After her second orgasm passed, Kitty clicked the vibrator off and laid it on his chest, pressing the tip of it up and into his mouth. Austin took it in his mouth, tasting Kitty's pleasure immediately, his cock responding almost emphatically, pressing against her still-throbbing clitoris.

"Does the bad boy think he's getting anything for Christmas?"

Austin smiled at her as she pulled the vibrator out of his mouth, pressing her own lips against his in a hard kiss. She pulled away from him but he could still see the pleasure subsiding in her eyes. Her body was tense yet relaxed at the same time, her arms still flexing from being locked in place during her orgasms.

"I just want the same thing you got."

Kitty just smiled and lifted up the candy cane vibrator.

"Really?"

Austin would have to remind himself that, from now on, he would need to be more specific in the bedroom. What he had simply meant was the receiving of orgasms from her through pleasure somehow translated in Kitty's mind to mean, 'Let's get playful with a vibrator in Austin's ass'.

Wrapping it up!
- The Morning After -

Fiery vixen under the covers, indeed! The defensive end felt Kittie's hips slam down onto his thighs as the sun came up in the nearby window, the tip of his member pressing up against the walls of her love cave, Austin moaning into the teddy bear pressed against his face, half-gasping as he felt the air from her body light his skin on fire again and again. The cinnamon-scented lotion she had poured on him earlier now burned his skin enough to make it painfully pleasurable, Kitty still scantily-clad in her X-mas costume, though her hair had fallen down around her now-bared breasts, a light sheen of sweat across her forehead and down her arms.

Kitty sucked on the end of the vibrator, her tongue lingering just a bit on the tip, enough for Austin to let out a deep breath, still urging this naughty little nymph forward until his climax could be felt. He found that he wanted to treat this hard-working girl like the slut she wanted to be tonight, finally giving into the idea of it fully as she writhed back against his legs again, the football player underneath feeling her tightening down on him harder than before.

That kitty is coming on me right now! And, as he looked up at her, her mouth opened wide in a frozen moan, her body jolting stiffly over him. She leaned forward a bit and dropped the candy cane onto the bed, her hands well placed on his chest as he felt her own pleasure spill down his cock and into his lap.

"Oh Austin, you naughty little boy! I'm coming…coming on you!" It was more of a whisper because Kitty still held her breath, the light fragrance of peppermint hanging over him for a moment longer.

Never in his life as a football player and stud had Austin Tagger taken such pleasure from a woman and gotten off on it! As she spoke those words, Austin's unsheathed member shook with delight and sprayed inside of her, her orgasm intensifying all the more.

"Ahh, fuck, Kitty!" But his voice was muffled, so it sounded more like, "Mmmph, fmmmmph, kmfmmmph!" to Kitty, who sat completely still now, the X-mas hat half-hanging from her head. Austin felt the velvet gloves come off her hands and fall onto his stomach, her hands lifting her off of him and down towards his thighs.

In another moment, he felt Kitty's tongue lapping up the orgasm dripping from his cock, her mouth taking in most of his still-stiff member as he shook in the aftershocks of pleasure.

Austin no longer protested the need to keep Kitty safe from naughty. After she took the teddy bear away from his head, Austin breathed in the mixed smells of the holidays and sex, which formed a new aroma all its own. Karen was back as well; the calmness in her eyes was there again. Kitty was gone for the moment, probably to bathe in the afterglow of her conquest, and the innocent-looking librarian stared meekly back out at him now, the kisses that she planted on his neck and chin soft and delicate.

"Happy Holidays, Austin Tagger!"

Karen had given him a gift. A gift that had never been wrapped so well, had never tasted so sweet, and had never felt so good to open and take delight in as Karen "Kitty" Meyers had been at that moment. From the simple outfit that held quite a bit of trouble underneath to the calmness in her eyes now, Austin regretted not a bit of it. And, as he fell asleep, finally untied from the bedposts, he dreamed of much more than just sugar plums that Christmas.

The End

Santa Claus needs love, too. ...The Naughty Kind!

Written by Titus Strong

CHAPTER ONE
-"WHAT A GLORIOUS DAY!"-

The winter snows in Traverse City, Michigan were something of a natural disaster themselves in that they brought about a whole new community experience when the snow fell, covering the landscape in a shitty mess, especially on the streets. Instead of the newly-fallen snow that you'd get in your yards and on your sidewalks and driveways, the mush that would sit atop an inch or two of water on the roads would remain throughout the holiday season.

Nathan Felders knew this from personal experience. Father of two and husband to a hot number that worked from home, he had become the practical parent and do-gooder from the get-go. When the snows came the first time, they were in their new home, he was sure to get every kind of machine to cut through snow that he could, even working with the local community to help on the sidewalks that went on for miles around them.

Yes, sir, that Nathan Felders was quite a guy.

However, Nathan was not just known for helping out with the snows when they fell upon Traverse City shortly after the Cherry Festival and the Summer Movie Marathons at the local theaters; he was a Christmas enthusiast to boot. He took pride in the fact that his house, on the block as well as throughout his entire neighborhood, was the most decorated house during the holiday season.

It wasn't the easy-to-assemble sort of decorations, either. Nathan was never a supporter of the inflated snow globes that sat in the lawn, more as a fixture than a symbol of what Christmas meant to him. He disliked that as well as the gaudiness that was making your entire yard a Christmas celebration, over-adorning everything on your property with lights.

Less is more, he had always thought to himself. And, indeed, he was right.

Tasteful Nativity Scene- Check!

Christmas Lights that outlined only the house- Check!

Santa, his sleigh, and the reindeer lit on the roof- Check!

Christmas wreath on the brightly wrapped front door- Check!

Yes, that Nathan Felders was a spirited guy!

Of course, his daily routine of working five days a week, spending time with the kids, adult time with his wife Ashley, as well as time with his buddies at work and his alumni group from college left little time to spruce up the decorations every year. He was always so caring and wanted to give to his children so much of what he didn't have himself whilst being a kid. His father had left his mother when he was just a boy to drink and womanize and Nathan hated the bastard ever since.

I'll never be that like. I'll never leave my family to exercise the sowing of wild oats after I'm already a grown man, Nathan thought to himself. However, he remembered a time before his marriage where he had gotten all of his sowing out of his system.

Ahhh, the college years. Amid the college syllabi, frat parties, and road trips that Nathan and his friends took in the four years he was in college, he had bedded many a woman.

Many of them were merely experiments for Nathan's budding manhood, while there were a select few that actually held real meaning over the years. Still, all in all, they were very decent lays and good stories that he could always pull from to spruce up any conversation with his old pals.

But the stories had been lacking as of late in regards to his bedroom banter; primarily because Nathan had allowed things to get a little stale; a little, simply put "for functional use only", spending far too much time on maintaining the status quo of his perfect life as the figure head of the Felders family and not taking the time to take off all the other "hats" in order to wear the wild hat of manhood to bed.

But that was all about to change this Christmas Eve.

However, before the merriment and festive fucking at the Felders' household begins, one must know what its like to be a parent during the holiday season.

On Christmas Eve, the two kids go to bed shortly after the dog does, father pretends to go to work and mom pretends to go to bed. (I'm sure you've heard something like this before.) The wife then helps the husband get the Santa suit on and fills Santa's bag with wrapped gifts and toys for the children. Mom checks about an hour later to make sure the coast is clear and Santa goes downstairs and posts himself outside the front door, acting as if he's delivering presents to the Felders family.

And when one says Santa suit, Nathan spared no expense. From head to toe, he looked like the Norman Rockwell Coca-Cola Santa of old, complete with rosy cheeks applied by the wife; the beard, (a glue-on so there would never be any doubt), and a real-deal buckled belt that held in the latex suit that threatened to spill out around Nathan's much smaller frame. There was no getting away from Santa Claus in the Felders' household, because he was a living, breathing, over-achieving father making up for his own father who had never been there.

So, here is where the wife's plan comes into play. Both parents have put in time making sure that Nathan always has to work on Christmas Eve and they even play up the importance of his role at work (though his company has always been closed during the Christmas holidays) and Nathan reluctantly leaves after tucking his kids into bed. He leaves and drives around the block until he gets a text from his wife that they are asleep, and then he sneaks back into his own house to get into costume. In the end, it was always worth keeping the kids in the Christmas spirit.

However, by this time, after years of putting the costume on and taking it off, Nathan could do it in his sleep and without his wife's help. Besides, there had been a few close calls in the past where the kids had woken up and both mom and dad were nowhere to be found. That gave the kids a chance to offer up their own ideas on where their parents were.

Nathan never wanted them to know during their childhood that their parents were actually Santa. He wanted them to simply grow out of it.

Like all kids should be able to do, Nathan reminded himself, slipping his car into the garage quietly. His wife had released the lever for manual override so he could open the garage door without the noise of the garage door opener, possibly waking the kids and alerting them that their father was home. The soon-to-be Santa closed the garage door behind him quietly and turned the lever back on, locking the door in place.

Nathan looked at the neatly organized garage and his shelving system that housed all of the extras in the home, including his Santa suit and all the pieces that he needed to make it a spot-on Rockwell Santa. He had smartly labeled two dark blue plastic totes **Dad's Tax files 1+2** making sure that the names bored his kids to no end so they would stay away from them. And putting the two totes on the top shelf helped as well. There was a third blue tote sitting next to the other two, labeled **Mom's Knitting Supplies**. But, again, it had been smartly labeled as something other than what was in the tote.

Ashley never knitted, Nathan reminded himself, pulling that tote down as well. He looked down into it. It was filled with the kid's presents, decorated with Santa wrapping paper, his Santa sack in the bottom of the tote, ready to be filled. Nathan pulled out all of his costume and placed the pieces in order of how they should be put on onto his work shelf, which had been cleared off weeks before just for this occasion.

Yes, the parents of the Felder family were a good team.

Chapter Two

-"What a glorious Night!"-

It was like a scene from a Lifetime TV Christmas special had come alive in their home. Nathan came through the garage door entrance and into the kitchen dressed as Santa, carrying his bag of gifts for both Emily and Carter, ages 6 and 8, tiptoeing his best Santa impersonation on through the dining room. Everything looked as it should.

There were beautifully crafted ornaments hanging on the tree for every family member.

Porcelain, limited edition from Lenox.

The tree was easily over seven and a half feet tall, nearly touching the ceiling in their living room.

Artificial Tree, Sears Ty Pennington Limited Edition. Retractable and easy to break down, with beautiful, white lights already crafted onto the Christmas tree itself. It takes me no time to put the tree up now.

There were rope lights wrapped around the staircase and the stockings were all hung 3-feet from one another, Nathan had made sure of that with his laser-level that he got a few Christmases back.

Everything looked perfect. All in place like it should be. Now to attend to these presents that I have in this bag.

There were nine presents in all. Two totes in the garage were full from the presents and, once Santa Claus had placed them in his merry Santa bag, he felt the joy of Christmas come alive within him. He couldn't help but smile time and again at the thought of his children opening these presents the following morning, even telling their father that they had seen Santa deliver the presents under the tree themselves.

Three special presents for each child, one present for the mother and father, and one present for the family to share together. Usually, the family gift encompassed board games, trips or vacations to different places they had never been before, and even gift packages of snacks, fruits, or Christmas candies. The Felder Household was sure to have a Merry Christmas every year.

So, when Santa came around the corner of the living room and saw a scantily clad wife Ashley Felders standing in stiletto heels of the stripper variety, the jolly old elf was a bit surprised.

And a bit hard, he took note, having to adjust his festive flesh underneath his belt.

Christmas-time Ashley looked like a perverted version of a Christmas Barbie doll. She wore a dress, though it was more of a skirt, which hung just low enough to cover her mama parts but let the cheeks of her ass poke out beneath the skirt, giving Santa something to hold on to, he would find out later. She wore a pair of black silk gloves that reached to the elbows and her red velvet corset hugged her hips even closer with a black Santa belt around her waist, her breasts nearly spilling out of the naughty attire.

Santa Claus Nathan stared in awe at his wife and mother of two.

"What are you doing, Ashley, its Christmas Eve! The kids will-"

But his wife simply moved closer to him, her gloved finger pressing against her husband's lips. She whispered to him. And the whisper sounded very little like his wife's voice, which made it easier for him to swallow down the idea she was about to hand him.

"Tonight, I'm not your wife, Nathan. Just like you're not my husband. You're Santa Claus, aren't you?" Nathan nodded silently. "So, tonight, I'm Santa's helper!"

Santa's helper ran her fingers through his white beard on his face and he could see a gleam in her eyes that looked on him now.

"I have something for Santa. I even took the time to wrap it."

Nathan decided to go along with the charade for the moment, using his best whispering Santa voice. "But I have toys to deliver, little helper!"

"The toys can wait!"

And then she unwrapped the most delicious and delightful gift Santa Claus had ever received. From the tight folds of her outfit, she pulled two strings and her breasts were freed from the corset and fell deliciously forward for Santa's waiting mouth.

The bag of toys quickly dropped to the floor, all responsibility suddenly forgotten for the moment. His bearded mouth was almost upon a hardened nipple when he felt Santa's helpers firm hand on him, pushing him back.

"I give it **to** you. **You take nothing**. That would be a naughty boy."

Already, Santa could feel his erection pressing hard against his red pants, urging to be a part of the action going on near the Christmas tree. But Santa's helper seemed to have a plan of her own. Being careful not to step on the bag of toys behind them, Santa was led over to one of the dining room chairs in the dining room not far away. There, he was made to sit down, his bulge now clearly defined and seen by the eyes on him.

"Oh, it looks like Santa has a present for me as well. Well, I'll get to that later. But first..."

Santa's helper pressed one of her breasts into his mouth, her fingernails digging into the bare skin of his neck, urging him forward, his bearded mouth suckling on it as he never had before.

Nathan didn't know how to feel about all of this. He knew that the toys still needed delivering, knew that he was the only one able to do it. He still needed to take the cookies they had baked for him, fill the stockings with care, wait for them to see him and then depart out just a quick as he had come, making sure that they saw no hint of their father or mother in the presentation at all.

In reality, for the first time in his life, he thought, *so this is how Santa feels! Always thinking of others and not himself. Always looking to the next house, the next gift under the tree, the next stocking to be stuff. What about Santa? Does he ever get to stuff the stocking of his choice?*

And the breasts in front of him looked even more tempting then, felt even more pleasurable than they ever had before. Maybe it was the fact that he was being given a chance to receive for once and not to have to give in return. Santa simply delighted in that fact and took the other nipple into his waiting mouth moments later.

"That's it! Good boy, Santa! You're getting the hang of this receiving thing quite well." There was something about those words of encouragement coming from his wife's mouth, something almost hypnotic about him being allowed to take and not be expected to give at all that made his erection all the harder. His body had become so accustomed to giving, to finding the spots and exploiting them, trying to outlast his partner with every precise thrust, that he had trouble allowing himself to be pleased without a response.

And that fact that she disguised her voice to sound different, to sound sultrier. It was almost as if Santa was fucking his little helper after all!

After a few moments, though, Santa's little helper pulled his bearded mouth away from the erect nipples, letting his tongue play with each of them a moment before she pushed Santa back into the dining room chair the rest of the way, covering up her breasts for the time being, other things on her mind.

Santa watched his little helper's eyes as they motioned onto the dining room table adjacent to his chair, a myriad of items on the top of the table, having replaced the cornucopia and the smaller decorations that had adorned their table for the last few weeks.

First, his little helper grabbed a pair of fuzzy, red handcuffs and walked around behind Santa's chair.

"We can't have Santa breaking the rules of the game, now can we? I'd have to have to punish you!" The whispers in his ear only presented a more visual future of the scenario at hand, with hopes that Santa could be in full motion behind his little helper, emptying out his warm eggnog out onto her ripe, juicy cantaloupe of an ass. This vision gave him the shivers slightly, his erection once again taking center stage, the bulge begging to be attended to.

"Actually, I wouldn't mind the punishing part. But I think we'd wake the little children, don't you?"

Nathan had never heard anything remotely naughty come from his wife's mouth in all his years. They had been naughty in the bedroom and she had even called him daddy or big poppa a few times during climax, but nothing out of the ordinary. Nothing like what he was hearing now.

Then came the blindfold. Soon, a satiny textured scarf wrapped around Santa's head, covering his eyes completely.

In a matter of moments, he could feel his little helper's hands at the great, black belt at his waist, soon smacking at his half-bare ass a little so he would lift up the rest of the way. Santa's red pants were now around his ankles, his erection out and in the open for the entire world to see. And then he heard his little helper's voice.

"Oh, Santa does have a present for me! How delightful." There was a moment of silence and then Santa felt the palm of his helper's hand teasing the head of his cock. He jolted back in surprise at how intense the feeling was, doing his best to control his response.

"My goodness, look at Santa. His face is turning red after just a touch. I'd hate to see what he'd do if I did this-" And that's when Santa's little helper took the entirety of Santa's cock in her mouth. From tip to shaft, Santa was engulfed in a sudden pleasure that made him moan out loud.

"Holy fucking mistletoe! That feels-" Santa couldn't finish his sentence.

Fuck, Santa didn't want to finish his sentence.

His merry self just sat there in his chair, handcuffed, blindfolded, receiving the most festive of blowjobs. By now, he was fully into the receiving mood. All thoughts of presents, cookies, and slipping out without being noticed had all melted away in his mind, his little helper beginning slow strokes with her mouth, letting Santa twitch and straighten up in his chair as many times as he needed to. He felt one hand grab for a hold onto his ass, the other wrapping itself around his shaft tightly, his little helper's lips contouring over every inch of his member, keeping great attention on the head of his candy cane until Santa was at full attention.

Santa's little helper said nothing for some time. Instead, she kept herself busy with Santa's slippery shaft and Santa didn't mind in the least. She was sure, though, that sugarplums weren't the only things that were dancing in the jolly old elf's mind. By the time she slowed her stroke down, Santa had a light sheen of sweat over his brow, his mouth making shapes and words that he dared not speak out loud.

Then came the naughty voice again.

"There are a couple more things I want for Christmas, Santa. What do I do, just sit on your lap and ask for them?"

Nathan simply nodded, trying to catch his breath, still watching the plump set of tits as they very nearly burst forth out onto his lap. Santa's little helper stood back up and turned around, her ass bare in front of him. She smiled from over her shoulder...

And then came another wave of pleasure as Santa felt his helper's ass press against his stomach, sitting herself down onto his rigid cock.

"My fucking goodness, you're being a bad girl!" Santa's little helper shifted ever so slightly, making sure that each inch of his pulsing candy cane was attended to properly, pressing her ass into his lap harder and harder each time.

Santa was sweating in his suit now. He had never worn the suit this long, let alone while getting fucked in it. Still, his pants were around his ankles, the light slapping of his helper's ass slamming down on him as she rode him with her back to him.

She had to take it slow without Santa's hands on her hips to keep her steady, for they were still handcuffed, still begging to be released. But the little helper didn't mind riding Santa on her own; she reached back and placed her hands on his shoulders and used her strong thighs to keep her floating just above Santa's goodies, pressing his festive rod deeper and deeper into her welcoming flesh.

"I want a pony for Christmas, Santa. I like riding things. Is that okay?" Now it was a little girl's pouty voice that came out of her mouth. He could almost envision her bottom lip sticking out as she took every inch of his jolly goodness into her, one hand moving to his thigh, the other soon falling onto his other thigh. His little helper rocked forward and that's when he could feel her other surprise; she was dripping wet with excitement.

A handcuffed Santa had turned his little helper on?

He decided to speak out against this, to continue the game.

"Looks like somebody has been a very naughty girl this year!"

He could feel her fingernails biting into the flesh in both his knees and his little helper had become silent all of a sudden.

She was concentrating. She was almost there herself.

"What else is on your list, little girl?"

But she didn't answer. She seemed far away now, her nails staying clenched, her rhythms a constant and almost in the same place every time. She held her breath.

This didn't seem to be part of the script at all, thought Jolly Old St. Nick, feeling beads of sweat dripping down onto him from her thighs. He felt her muscles getting tired in her legs. But she was bringing him close to his merry load as well. Already, he could feel the full stirrings of pleasure jolting forward to be felt, his eyes closing beneath the blindfold, taking in the experience of his little helper doing all the work.

"Little girl, are you okay? Do you need some help getting off on Santa's lap?"

Santa thrust deep then, his little helper bouncing up a bit in surprise. But Santa knew exactly how to set his little helper off. Already, the pleasure erupted around his merry member, her hands tightening around his knees, her ass still and floating just above his thighs.

"There it is, Santa! Just what I wanted for Christmas. All over you." The little girl voice had disappeared. Santa could hear a sultry woman's voice answering him back. And it didn't feel like his little helper's body wanted to play games anymore. What had become a fun and entertaining romp in Christmas décor had become something of a more serious nature.

"You don't play fair, Santa." Santa could hear the vindictive nature of her words trying to cut through the game but still retaining a little bit of the helper's persona.

"Better not pout." His little helper climbed off of him then, taking off the blindfold and handcuffs. Santa stretched out his sore limbs and reached for the little helper then, his black gloves almost slipping off her thighs that were still wet with desire and hard work.

"Gonna find out who's naught and nice?" She continued with the game, though the little helper's eyes were glossed over with post-coital pleasure.

"Santa Claus is coming-" His little helper grabbed him by the hand led him over to the Christmas Tree.

"-right now!"

His little helper bent over, her ass exposed, her warm little fireplace alive and on fire from their last encounter. Santa steadied himself near the presents under the tree and slid into her easily, his gloved hands grabbing for her hips underneath the naughty attire she wore.

"There's one last present, isn't there, Santa?" His little helper turned back to him and smiled, biting her lip as he plunged in deeper and deeper, hitting spots she had not allowed him to before.

"Yes, little helper, there is. And I want to give it to you."

"Then give it to me, Santa!"

And, being in such a festive and jovial mood, Santa did just that. It wasn't long before the jolly old elf gripped his little helper's hips even tighter, holding onto the holiday feeling the best he could.

"I'm almost there, little helper!"

By this time, Santa was about to explode. He could feel his special gift welling up inside him, the quick, fluid movements being made even more fluid with the lubrication his little helper had put on his festive holiday member, sliding in and out of her, increasing the sensitivity an easy sevenfold. Santa's little helper, though panting now, turned back to look at him as he pressed on, Santa on the verge.

"Are you going to give me a present, Santa? Will it be a White Christmas after all?"

As the naughtiest of naughty lines escaped his wife's lips, he knew he couldn't contain himself any longer. Grabbing onto his helper's hips tightly, he plunged in one last time, his orgasm thundering out of him.

"Oh, oh, oh!" Santa shook with delight, emptying out the contents of his goody sack into his little helper's warm fireplace, his black gloves grabbing at her outfit for a firm hold as he let the joy of the Christmas season subside within him. He was just about to pull out when he heard a familiar set of voices call out to him from the steps.

"Santa, what are you doing to mommy?" Two children sat atop the steps, watching them in their holiday escapades.

No telling how long they had been watching. Now, the only tricky thing to get out of was how Santa and his little helper were going to compose themselves after such an intense moment.

As the post-coital smoke cleared, Nathan had an idea. Putting on his best Santa voice, he said, "I was thanking your mother for the wonderful cookies, little boy. Now, go back to bed and you'll have some wonderful presents under the tree in the morning."

The two kids were reluctant at first, but bought the act, moving themselves back upstairs quietly.

Nathan pulled out of his little helper and began to pull up his Santa trousers when a hand reached out for him to stop. Santa's little helper smiled again, moved closer, and began kneading his ass, teasing his semi-hard member with her tongue.

"Santa feel like two presents tonight?"

Santa smiled his jolly old smile and continued until late into the night, ensuring that all his presents were delivered, emptying out his sack once more for the little helper, who was oh-so-kind enough to receive it.

The End

# Christmas Eve With Steve

Written by Titus Strong

CHAPTER ONE
-AND YOU THOUGHT
GEORGE BAILEY'S NIGHT WAS ROUGH! -

Stephen Teller knew that this day would come. He knew that he would one day wake up a New Jersey gutter, smelling of piss and liquor. He just never thought it would be on Christmas Day. The twenty-eight-year-old tried to recount the events of the previous night only to discover that he couldn't, finding himself without a single memory of what had happened.

I must have had an awful fucking Christmas, Stephen thought to himself, shivering from the cold. It was still snowing, the flakes coming down on him lightly, his jacket and face blanketed in the stuff.

There's at least five inches of snow on the ground! How did I survive out here in the cold? This and a great many things he pondered as he picked himself up off the curb, hobbling home, what he soon realized was nearly a two-mile hike from where he lived, the apartment he shared with his roommate Trent. His jacket had kept him somewhat warm during the trek back but, as he neared his apartment, he was freezing cold.

What the fuck happened to me last night?

In mere moments, Stephen Teller would soon find out.

After breaking the chill from two miles outside in 30-degree weather, Stephen managed to shake the snow off him and make it up the stairs of his complex, fiddling with the contents in his pockets until he unleashed his keys upon the door, pushing the door open with his free hand. Stephen looked around the apartment for any signs of his roommate.

Must have already left for the holidays to be with his family, Stephen thought, making his way straight through the living room and kitchen to his room and, upon shedding his pissed-scented clothing on the floor, made a "the-house-is-fucking-chilly" sprint to his bathroom, where he showered fiercely. The smell as well as the ache from the cold soon came off his body in waves, Stephen taking some time to let the steam relax the soreness out of his limbs. It wasn't until he was nearly finished showering that he noticed a condom still on his flaccid member below.

"What the fuck?" *It was there, all right.*

Stephen shook his head in disbelief and, as he took it off, he noticed that it had been used quite well on his end at least, noting a hefty amount of his little white soldiers still left in the latex. He dropped it in the toilet just outside the shower and scrubbed himself with a good lathering of soap, trying his best to recall again what had occurred the night before.

I don't remember shit from last night! What the fuck happened?

Nonetheless, exhaustion kicked in and ruled his sorry ass once he got out of the shower, knowing that he needed to rest before going to see his family, which were a few miles away in Paramus, New Jersey. So, he did the best he could at drying off and was about to fall off into a great and mighty slumber when he noticed a still form in his bed. Except that, as he moved closer, the form was not so still.

A woman he had never met, an attractive one at that, shifted in her place on his bed, lifting herself and her gorgeous breasts up for him and the entire world to see. However, Stephen was glad that the entire world was not there in his room because he wanted to enjoy this sight all by himself.

He knew little of her height and the rest of her body from the waist down because it was still covered with his sheets, but from the waist up she was an eyeful.

Then she spoke.

"Stevie, I thought you were going out to get breakfast for us? I'm starving after what we did last night. What happened to you?"

She smiled and giggled a little, which made her perky tits bounce a bit, Stephen already beginning to feel the stirrings of an erection taking hold beneath his towel.

"Hi....um..yeah, about last night."

"Oh, Stevie, you want to talk about last night? Holy shit, what were you on? You fucked me three ways from Tuesday with that cock of yours!"

"Wow! That's great to know. I am just having trouble..."

Fucked her three ways from Tuesday? What the fuck is this about?

"Oh, come here, you naughty boy! Farah will take care of any problem you have!"

And, with that, the newly acquired Farah pulled herself free from Stephen's covers and moved over to this so-called Stevie that Stephen knew nothing about and pulled the towel free from his waist, letting it drop to the floor and fall down with the other items that Stephen knew very little about on his own bedroom floor.

It was all of her clothes from last night. She slept here… and we fucked… in my bed!

"Oh, it looks like he's up for a rematch, huh, Stevie? I'm down for that," taking his cock in her mouth and pressing it deep into her throat, she pulled away, smiling at him, "if you know what I mean!"

And Stephen undoubtedly knew what she meant after seeing that look in her eyes. Many women don't get that look, he noticed, Stephen filing away that look that Farah gave him just then for a lonely moment in the future that he tried his best not to think about right now. Very few women will be dirty, will talk dirty, and act dirty in the bedroom without some kind of commitment.

But Farah...

It seemed rather easy for this so-called Stevie she was talking about to allow Farah to take his cock into her mouth, especially after the description of the kind of night they had, anyway. And, hopefully for Stephen, this would jar his memory of the great sex that they had the night before and he would remember more than just this blowjob-and whatever came next.

She moved her long, brown tassels of hair from her face so Stevie could see her mouth take in the head of his dick, her lips devouring it immediately, the new and improved Stevie trying his best to keep his eyes open, though they urged for him to close and enjoy all of the oral delights this delicious-looking beauty was bestowing upon him.

In those moments afterward, Farah treated him like a stallion and rode his newly showered self back to dirtiness; something Stephen had trouble imagining without the actual visual image in front of him. In what lasted the span of 27 minutes, Stevie showed himself to be quite a lady killer, invoking the long-lost spirit of some dead porn star in this chance encounter with Farah, barely filling up his desire cup after his first orgasm. Well, his first remembered orgasm with her.

The first time didn't count because I don't remember it.

This was one of his newly made rules and he was sticking to it.

This one counted. This one, this awesome one that she just gave me, looking over at the panting Farah beside him, *this counts.*

"Babe, I'm hungry. I thought you were going to get us breakfast hours ago."

Hours ago? How long had Farah been here? All night?

"How long have you been here?"

Farah slipped the covers up over her exposed breasts, her nipples still perky from the sex they just had as well as from the cold chill that had set in on the two of them.

"All night. I guess.... what, since about three a.m., when you picked me up at the strip club."

Strip club? Stephen's cock did a double take.

Did we just fuck a stripper, asked Stephen's semi-hard dick, wobbling loosely between his legs.

"You were there with friends, right Farrah; a bachelorette party or something?" He tried to play off that he wasn't excited about the possibilities. He hoped that this wasn't her answer. Rebounding from his break-up with Angela over the Christmas Holiday with a stripper would be most excellent and well-deserved first step of recovery for him.

Farah just looked at him somewhat wildly and threw his covers off, exposing the rest of her body, standing up in the dimly lit room.

"The thermostat is over here, right?"

Stephen nodded and waited for a response. The heat kicked on and soon he could feel the warmth coming back to the room. He didn't know if it was from what he had just done with this gorgeous creature or from the heater, but he didn't mind either at the moment.

"You're being silly, Stevie. You waited until I got off work last night before you hit on me, remember?"

We fucked a stripper! Stephen's dick leapt for joy under the covers.

But the semi-blank stare that Stephen gave her tipped her off immediately.

"Wow, you don't remember anything, do you?" She paused, slipping back into the bed with him. "Well, I can completely understand. You got fucked up last night with your friends. Your friends said you were nursing some break up...some girl named-"

Stephen finished the sentence for her. "-Angela. Yeah. She broke up with me yesterday and cancelled the trip with me to meet my parents."

Farah cuddled up to Stephen then, running her hands through the small trail of hairs that lay upon his chest.

"That's fucked up! What kind of person does that to somebody?"

"I know, right! I was crushed."

"Had Angela ever met your parents before?"

"No, not yet."

"How long had you guys been going out?"

"Almost a year. Just a little after Christmas last year, just after New Year's Eve."

The room was quiet for a moment. They both listened to one another breath as the heat continued to filter warm air into the room.

It was nice to just to exist for the moment, the recently made Stevie thought decidedly, squeezing Farah closer to him. Then the thought popped into his mind.

"I have no fucking idea where my wallet is."

It was in those moments when stripping down to take a shower that he noticed. His wallet usually fell out of his back jeans pocket and onto the floor. When it didn't, he didn't think anything of it, getting into the shower to clean the stink of the night before off of him. It wasn't until just now that he had cleared his mind enough to take notice.

"You have any idea where my wallet could be?"

"I don't remember seeing it when we took a cab this morning. But I paid this morning because you bought the drinks last night. You may have left it at the club."

Though Stephen would love to spend the rest of Christmas Day fucking the shit out of a stripper named Farah, he knew that he needed to be the responsible one.

After all, there was no way he would be able to get on that bus later today to visit his family without his i.d. And he didn't want to deprive this beauty of something to eat, even though there were several things that he wouldn't mind putting in her mouth besides food. He stored away that idea for later and, rather reluctantly, got out of bed to look for his missing wallet.

He pulled an emergency twenty-dollar bill from his bedside drawer and grabbed his iPhone and left the burlesque beauty named Farah naked in his bed, dressing for the cold quickly, his boots soon echoing down the front steps and out of his place, a small layer of snow crunching under his feet.

How the fuck did I survive out in this weather last night, Stephen thought to himself, hurrying the best he could to meet with the Uber on the corner of his street before the light changed. An older model Honda Civic pulled up and a wrinkly old man smiled out at him.

"Stephen," the old man questioned. Stephen nodded and slipped into the back seat. He had gotten the name of the strip club from Farah before he left and hoped beyond all hope that his wallet laid snuggly between a set of oiled up breasts, keeping it warm for his return.

"To the Lion's Den, on Channing Street."

The Uber pulled off.

Chapter Two
- Into the Lion's Den -

The Lion's Den was something of a mess of a strip club, Stephen knew, for he had been several times early in his college years. But he had not been back since then. He only hoped that it had changed, for none of the previous night was coming back to him at all. Even with no symptoms of a hangover now, he couldn't remember a single thing.

But last night at the strip club was not to be taken lightly. What Stephen had gone in to do with his buddies (which was wallow in pity by having overpriced drinks because his girlfriend broke up with him that morning) turned into something much more than revenge or pity sex. Single-handedly, Stephen had apparently turned into the shining cock-knight of old. His early college years, which had been spent in establishments such as this strip club as well as local bars that smelled of piss and, well, piss, had become some of his spots where he would pick up an intellectual hottie or two with but a bit of banter.

It wasn't difficult to do at all. He wasn't buff or rich or even owned a nice car or had a pair of shoes over $100 dollars, but he was in the transition phase. For those of you who do not know what the transition phase is, enlightenment on this exact subject is quickly approaching via next paragraph.

Enlightenment is when, in one great swoop, you are finding your identity, moving away from your parents, finding your sexuality, stretching your credit as well as your abilities as an individual all the while trying to maintain an existence in the world and make a name for yourself. Stephen's name at the moment, which stuck out in his head right now when he thought of the stripper in his bed only moments from this moment in the Uber, was Stevie.

Apparently, Stevie had done something Stephen had never done before. And to a stripper no less!

This last little tidbit of information would keep him as legend status among his friends and co-workers when he came back from Christmas break after the weekend was over.

He smiled at the thought of this, not thinking so much on his ex-girlfriend, their happy times together; but more on the blowjob given to him earlier and the breakfast he was about to get once he got his wallet back from the strip club.

Yes, Christmas Day was going quite well; much better than Christmas Eve. He approached the strip club with a little spring in his step as he got out of the Uber, looking on the possibilities as endless, all because of a piece of random ass that brightened his melancholy spirit.

"You know what, little man? You need to get the fuck out of here before I call the cops on your ass!"

This wasn't the best welcome that he gotten at the front doors of a strip club before, but it would have to be the most interesting. Stephen was surprised at the response that the bouncer gave him when he tried to get into the club a few minutes later, having the Uber wait for him just outside the club.

"What are you talking about, man? I just want my wallet back!"

"After all the damage that you caused, you're lucky I don't have you arrested! The owner had mercy on you, you piece of shit!"

The 275-pound plus bouncer puffed up at the chest then, Stephen easily shrinking back into wuss mode as he was so accustomed to being in most of the time.

But there was a naked, sexy stripper in my bed, waiting for me to get her some breakfast and do a great many nasty things that I don't even have time to think about right now! It was time for this Stevie to think, and think fast!

"Farah sent me."

"What?" The bouncer was caught off guard with the name.

"Farah. You know, she works here!"

"I know she works here, dipshit! Why are you bringing her up?"

Just then, an older gentleman in a cheap three-piece suit stepped through the door and eyeballed Stephen but said nothing.

"Because she's at my house right now crashed out in my bed. She wants some breakfast and I need my wallet."

Stephen had no idea that name alone would lead to a punch in the face, which it did, making him reel back in surprise, grabbing his nose in the process. He smelled the blood before he felt it running out of his nose and down into his mouth, Stephen doing his best to keep on his feet as the bouncer moved towards him, ready to strike again.

"Motherfucker! That's my girl you're talking about!"

Oh shit! The stripper I fucked is the bouncer's girl!

Stephen had seen this in the movies but never really thought it would play out in front of him in real life.

"Dude, I didn't know! I was so fucked up last night!"

But the bouncer didn't seem to care or want an explanation.

"Well, you're about the get fucked up today, too, you little fucker!"

Stephen wasn't by any means a little guy. Coming in at 5ft. 11in. and 185 pounds, he wasn't completely useless as a man. But, when compared to the bouncer and just the sheer thickness of his arms, Stephen could see himself being snapped in half easily over a Big Mac, so he could only imagine what the bouncer had in mind when approaching him because of his stripper girlfriend.

Then the older gentleman stepped into the situation, holding his hand up to the bouncer.

"Big Jake, calm down." The older gentleman's voice was smooth and calm and made Big Jake calm as well because he stopped his movement towards Stephen.

"This motherfucker is about to get it, John!"

John acknowledged the situation but waved his bouncer back.

"Let this guy get his wallet and get the fuck out of here. You can call Farah and deal with **that** situation later. We don't want this kind of business happening here, especially at the front door. For Christ's sake, what are you thinking?"

The place had changed. There used to be fights in the parking lot all the time. Maybe it's not so bad of a place as it had been all those years ago.

"Big Jake, get it for him. It's in the lost and found box. Lucy found it last night and brought it to me this morning."

"But what about-"

John lifted an eyebrow and the great beast named Big Jake nodded.

"I'll take your place until you come back with it."

Big Jake moved from his place, taking a quick 'Go fuck yourself' glance back at Stephen as he went in through the two double doors that had a great set of metal lion heads on them, disappearing behind them.

John, the owner, cut a slight smile at the corner of one side of his mouth.

"So, you got lucky last night, huh, pal?"

Stephen was still feeling the punch in the face but he had enough sense to know when to say when.

Shit, Farah might be his girlfriend, too.

But Stevie wasn't a coward. And, somewhere, deep down inside Stephen guessed, Stevie allowed himself to be shown, just a little bit at first.

"Well, let's just say I wasn't unlucky."

"Farah is a nice piece of ass, that's for sure. She's not to be disrespected. She has a good head on her shoulders. That girl is going places."

Stephen wondered how many times the owner had said that about his strippers, only to watch them wash away their youth on his stage at night. But Stephen didn't want to think about that gorgeous stripper in his bedroom wasting away. If anything, he wanted to get some food inside her and spend a little bit more "quality time" before he had to leave to visit his family.

In another few moments, Big Jake was back and the strange glare that John had been giving him was soon assuaged, Stephen getting his wallet back without having to have stitches. But Big Jake couldn't hold himself back from having the last word.

"Motherfucker, I don't forget a face! Or a name!"

Big Jake threw Stephen's wallet at him, Stephen catching it full force in the chest.

"Thank you, Big Jake."

"Fuck you, you little punk!" And, at that moment, for some unknown reason, Stevie came out to play.

"Awww, where's your Christmas spirit, Jakey boy?"

Stevie walked back over to his waiting Uber and slid in the back.

And Stevie decided it would be best to get the last word in. "I'll tell Farah you said hi."

Big Jake started his sprint towards the Honda Civic just as it drove off, Stevie giving him the bird as the vehicle moved further down the street, Jake breathing heavily, barely outside of the parking lot of The Lion's Den.

"Merry Christmas, you fat fuck!" Stevie called out, leaning back into the Uber, the old man in the car laughing hysterically at his antics.

"You are one crazy motherfucker, mister!"

Stevie smiled, still feeling the sting of the punch he had received just a few minutes earlier. Already, it was difficult to breath out of his nose without a sharp, shooting pain lighting up behind his eyes.

"Fuck it, it's the holidays!" Stevie rubbed his wound lightly, looking back one last time to see the roof of The Lion's Den disappear from sight. The Uber driver slapped his steering wheel enthusiastically.

"That's what I'm talking about! That's the way to live, mister!"

Stevie smiled through his temporary pain and remembered why he had traveled back to the strip club. He opened his wallet and was surprised to see a stack of fifty-dollar bills, close to $500 dollars in cash inside, whereas he was only expecting to find two twenties.

They weren't even in there at all. But Stevie wasn't complaining, not in the least.

"Well, I'll be fucked! It **IS** beginning to look a lot like Christmas after all!"

Chapter Three

~ "Oh, the Weather Outside is Frightful…" ~

"What do you mean, you go as Angela? Are you crazy or something?" Stephen couldn't believe what he was hearing. Both he and Farah sat at a diner not far from his apartment, watching as the snow came down in blankets around them.

It had started to snow harder ever since I left The Lion's Den, Stephen thought, looking at the nearly empty diner and its few occupants dotting the booths not far from him and the stripper-turned-comfort-rebound.

The Pancake Plaza was a rip-off of Waffle House mixed with a little bit of marketing stolen from International House of Pancakes thrown in to keep it from being sued by just one company. They even had an old jukebox that played digital hits flashing in the corner of the place. Farah had put in a few dollars and the song that had just started was one of Stephen's favorites; *Lullaby* by The Cure.

"Listen for a second, dipshit! Man, you don't let someone get a word in edgewise, do you?"

She was right. I hadn't shut up throughout most of the conversation.

"The way I see it is this; both of us are off for Christmas. You've got a bus trip to take; your girl ditched you. You've got an extra ticket, right?"

"Yeah."

My dumb ass bought both of our tickets as part of a Christmas gift for her.

"Well, did you tell your parents that she isn't coming yet?"

Stephen shook his head.

"And have they seen pictures of this Angela girl yet?"

He shook his head again.

"Well, I could totally be her then, right?"

Stephen chewed on some eggs and took a long swallow of coffee before speaking.

"I guess you could be."

"Well, that settles it."

"Settles what, exactly?"

"I can be your date for your parent's Christmas dinner **and** you can save face in front of all of your family at the same time. It's a win-win situation!"

Stephen couldn't help but think of the idea as genius, especially coming from a stripper. And the idea of pulling off something like this and getting a huge one-up on his two older brothers by bringing in someone as sexy as Farah with him as arm candy would give him newfound respect that he wouldn't ever have gotten with the real Angela.

Stephen had one problem. It was actually a 275-pound problem with raging anger issues.

"What about Big Jake? Would he be happy with the idea of you going to meet some other guy's family for Christmas?"

Farah's eyes darted to Stephen quickly then down to her coffee, where they stayed for a time while she drank the rest of her cup. She answered him minutes later.

"He's more there for protection than anything else. He has a crush on me and I don't feel like getting manhandled every night by a bunch of drunks - case closed."

"Well, he has a different take on things than you do, I'm afraid. He punched me in the face when I mentioned your name and where you were."

"He did what?" Farah's voice was a bit louder than Stephen would have liked it to be, the few patrons at the diner turning around to see who had made the commotion around them. Their eyes stayed on Farah for only a moment and then drifted back to wherever they had been before that.

"Keep it down, will ya! I'd like to come back here sometime soon!"

"He hit you?"

"In the face. Right in the nose, actually. Hurt like a motherfucker!"

"Did you put ice on it to keep the swelling down?"

"Do strip clubs even have ice?"

"Yes, they do. You can get it from the bartender."

"Well, they very well wouldn't let me go inside the strip club to get my wallet, let alone to get some ice for my nose when your boyfriend punched me!"

"They wouldn't let you in? Why not?"

"Something about the damage that I did last night with some of my friends."

"You didn't do any damage last night, well not while I was there."

"Well, apparently, I went back."

"Went back? After you picked me up and took me home with you?"

"I think so. It's slowly but surely starting to come back to me now. I do remember going back but not being able to get back in because I didn't have my I.D. because I left it with the bartender."

"So, you had your wallet but didn't have your I.D. after you fucked me and went out for breakfast?"

"Not to my knowledge."

"Wow, it seems you had a pretty crazy night! Well, at least you got back in one piece."

"By the way, when we had sex, did we use protection last night?"

"Yeah, of course we did. We're both strangers to one another. Why would we be that intimate so quickly?"

Now this was the part that I had second thoughts about. What if the condom wasn't from Farah and I but from someone else altogether?

But Stephen had to allow this to run its course. So far, all he had gotten was a punch in the face.

Farah was finishing up her pancakes. She took a sip of her orange juice and looked at him quizzically.

"Why do you ask?"

"I kind of found a used condom on me this morning when I took a shower. I had no idea that it was there."

Farah paused in finishing her pancakes. She looked up at him and smiled. It was a very naughty smile she gave to him.

"So, what you're saying is; you went out with your boys, got trashed, brought me back home and fucked the shit out of me, left out for a very early breakfast, went back to the strip club, and probably ended up partying, having more sex with another stripper, got kicked out of a strip club for being rowdy and came back for seconds with me?"

"Yep, that sounds about right."

"Is there anything else that I'm missing in this?"

"Yes. I woke up in the gutter and didn't know how I got there."

"In a gutter?"

"Two miles from my house. And I had to walk home."

"Wow, Stevie! When you break it off with a girl, you really break it off! Way to purge and get that shit out of your system!"

"You're not mad?"

Farah took a hefty bite from what was left of her pancakes and washed it down with a splash of coffee from her cup. She countered while still chewing the last of her pancakes.

"Am I you're girlfriend? No! Did we have great sex last night? Yes! And you've been quite the gentleman and not a complete douche after last night, so I'm kind of winging it with you right now to see how it goes."

"And that's what you're basing things on right now?"

"What else is there to base it off of, Stevie? We don't really know each other and you wouldn't believe how many assholes I've ended up with, thinking they were a nice guy like you and finding out that they weren't any better than a one night lay. Maybe not even worth that."

"I see your point. And what about Big Jake?"

"He's just a big baby in my book. I wouldn't worry about him too much. He'll blow off some steam tonight on some poor innocent guy that looks like you and toss him out into the street and he'll be fine in a couple of days."

At that point, Stephen became somewhat reflective, taking in all that had been said after he got his coffee refilled by the waitress who came by.

Angela is gone. My Christmas is pretty much shot, with the exception of Farah and her early Christmas gift of some rebound sex. I've already been punched and threatened by a guy that could eat me for breakfast, lunch, and dinner and he would still be hungry for more. And, if I go to my parent's house without my girlfriend, I'll get the pity treatment from my parents and made fun of by my brothers.

What else do I have to lose?

Both Farah and Stephen talked for a bit longer and, as the snow came down around them just outside the window, Stephen opted to get going sooner rather than later, before it got any more worse outside.

"Well, if you really want this to happen, I think we need to leave sometime soon."

Farah's face lit up.

"Really? You're really gonna let me go with you?"

"Sure, Farah." Stephen motioned with his outstretched hands at all the Christmas décor hanging on the walls in the diner. It's Christmas."

Farah reached across the table and grabbed his face up in her hands, kissing him hard on the lips. This and the fact that Farah's skimpy outfit showed off a bit of flesh at that angle got the patrons and waitresses attention and there was soon a round of applause all around the two of them.

After embarrassing Stephen while at the same time giving him mad diner points for the next time that he showed his face in there, he continued.

"The snow is coming down pretty hard out there and we don't want to be standing out in it when it's time for the bus to get here. The line for that thing is sometimes pretty long and, after about the 10th person, there's no more room under the canopy to stay warm and dry. I think we need to leave soon."

Chapter Four

"Let it snow, let it snow, Let it snow!" -

Warm and dry. Isn't that what all people want on a cold, Christmas night without family and friends around?

Apparently so.

Shortly after leaving the diner and grabbing Stephen's bags from his place while his stripper friend took a shower and freshened up, they pulled up at the bus station in a cab, looking out at the line of people already waiting for the bus.

All in all, they were number 35 and 36 in line, standing out in the cold, the snow coming down more than before, sticking to the ground in wet, half-melting patches that created slush and mush underneath their feet.

Farah was lucky enough to be clad in winter wear, though Stephen had seen the outfit underneath as well as the skimpy items that clung to her slim hips and busty frame up top.

She looked like a cute little snow bunny now, Stephen thought to himself, shaking the bags in his hands to keep the snow from accumulating on them.

"What are your parents like, anyway?" Farah began, moving in place to keep warm, blowing into her gloved hands to keep the cold away.

"That's a good question. I've been trying to figure that out for years and I still don't know."

They shared a smile again. They had been sharing a few of those tonight, this one coming out rather easily.

"I don't know. Normal, I guess. My dad worked at a mill for 20 years and retired shortly after that to start his own hardware store. My mom, she was a housewife that turned her candle parties into a lucrative business. She travels a lot and has fun doing it. They're both in good shape; they don't have cancer or any diseases that are dragging them down. I guess they're kind and from humble beginnings."

"Good description!"

"Thanks. What about yours?"

There was a slight pause before Farah answered.

"Me. Oh, not so lucky. You know, the sad stripper story where she comes from a bad family unit, she runs away early on in her teens to get away and hides her contempt for the world around her with a smile as she gets tipped $20 dollar bills between her breasts. Yeah, that's pretty much my story."

"Wow, I'm sorry, Farah. I didn't know."

She didn't look as though she needed any sympathy or wanted any.

"I've been getting by fine on my brains and good looks. I don't really need them anyway. They always weighed me down."

"So, what do you usually do during the holidays, catch a ride with a stranger on the bus to visit strange families?"

She sighed. "No. I usually volunteer for the Christmas shift at the place I work and get paid the extra bucks for working holidays."

"Good plan. Capitalizing on the holidays. That would be me too except that I had this trip planned to do the big reveal of the girlfriend and all."

"Sounds like both our holidays are sucking this year overall, huh, Stevie?"

What Stephen saw in her eyes made Stevie come out in him with fierceness then. He reached out in the snow-filled space between them and grabbed her, pulling her close. He kissed her and she kissed him back, the air nearly knocked out of her by the force he had pulled her to him.

The bus turned the dimly lit corner of the street and was soon upon them.

Farah's eyes were glazed over and she was near panting, her hands grabbing at his winter coat to keep him close. The line moved around them. Stevie stood there with her a moment longer.

"What was that for, Stevie?"

"A thank you for all that you've done."

"That was a damn good thank you!"

They shuffled in on the bus and shook their coats off before they seated, feeling the draft of the open bus door as they took their seats without their bulky winter coats on.

Stephen motioned to their seats.

"Aisle or window?"

Farah was still putting up her coat in the overhead storage.

"What?"

"Would you like the aisle or window seat?"

"Window would be nice."

Stephen waited for Farah to get comfortable in the window seat, sitting himself down on the aisle seat next to her.

Once the remaining passengers got on, the bus was away and they were on their way to his family's house. Farah pressed up against Stephen's shoulder and was soon fast asleep.

But John's words echoed in Stephen's head most of the ride. 'Farah is a nice piece of ass, that's for sure. She's not to be disrespected. She has a good head on her shoulders. That girl is going places.' The young man's nose was still swollen a little and he had trouble breathing through it. Hopefully, the swelling would go down considerably before he arrived at his parent's house.

Where did John think she was going? A good head on her shoulders? Nothing that Farah had said about herself seemed to match up with what John had been saying, unless he was talking complete and utter bullshit at that moment just to humor a stranger, Stephen thought to himself, Farah pressing her body up against him then in a desperate attempt for warmth.   All that man had said wouldn't stop Stephen from enjoying her company, which he had been ever since he found her naked in his bed that morning.

Wonder what my family will think? Will they really believe that this woman is Angela? Stephen didn't have much more time to think about it because, in another few moments, he was soon fast asleep, too, resting his head atop Farah's in a sex-induced, belly full of food sleep coma.

*   *   *

"Steve! Steve, my man!" Stephen woke up to the sound of his name and a slight shaking by an unknown hand. He shook his head so his eyes could become adjusted to the darkness around him, still coming to terms that he was on the slow-moving bus on Christmas Day. And there, in front of him, was a complete stranger trying to shake him awake.

"Can I help you?" Stephen did his best to use his toughest voice, but him just waking from sleep didn't help with the toughness at all.

"Holy shit, it's Steve, guys! Check it out!" The stranger motioned to others sitting around him to Stephen and they all cried out in unison.

"**STEVE!!!!!!!**" The cheer broke the silence of the bus and woke all sleeping passengers near them. Then the strangers that knew him said their individual hellos.

"What's up, buddy?" A shadowed but friendly face said.

"Have a good night?" Another voice called out in the dark.

"Holy hell, we never thought we'd see you again after you got kicked out last night!"

Stephen tried to remember their voices, the faces he could see, or recall any of what they were talking about, but drew a blank.

"I'm sorry guys, but what are you talking about?"

The first stranger that had spoken to him continued.

"It's me, Mitch; from Terrence's bachelor party. You honestly don't remember us?"

"I wish I could say that I did."

"Aww, man! You got tore up last night with us. You were crazy!"

"At The Lion's Den?"

"YEAH, MAN! Now you're talking!" Mitch called to the others.

"He remembers now, guys." A cheer came from their side of the bus.

"Yeah, Steve. We thought you got arrested or something after the show because we didn't see you at all and the bouncer wouldn't tell us where you went. Eventually, we had to leave in the limo to take Terrence back so he could get rest before his wedding. We're just now leaving the wedding reception."

And, as Stephen looked at Mitch closer, he could see the white tuxedo dress shirt that he sported, an untied tie hanging loosely from around his neck.

The bus had apparently been traveling for hours now, unbeknownst to Stephen and Farah. The bus rolled into a populated rest area with a small chain of restaurants connected by an interior plaza. The bus driver called out as he stopped.

"Thirty minutes, ladies and gentlemen. We'll re-board shortly after that." The bus driver opened the hydraulic doors and climbed down the few steps and out into the cold, bundling himself up for the snow that was still falling all around them.

Mitch nudged Stephen. "Hey, Steve! Get off here with us, you and your friend. We'll buy you something to eat and tell you more about it."

Over Dunkin Donuts coffee and a few late-night breakfast sandwiches, Mitch and the others related to Stephen and Farah what had happened the night before. After they were finished, the bachelor party fellows walked the two of them outside and offered them the hit off a joint. Both Farah and Stephen took it gratefully.

Stephen was the first one to respond.

"So, you mean to tell me that I snuck in with your bachelor party last night, posed as one of the bachelors, drank with you all, got lap dances, and started a fight with some stranger all in one night?"

The bachelor party pack all nodded their heads in unison.

Farah spoke up.

"Did he fuck anybody while he was there?"

The bachelor crew shook their heads.

"Not that we know of, Farah. He was pretty much hanging out with us the entire time at the club. The only one that got laid was the groom-to-be."

Stephen was wary about mentioning the money he had found in his wallet but he wanted to know where it came from, even if he would have to give it back. To have some closure over all the pieces of the night before is something he valued more than anything else at the moment.

"What about the money? How did I get the money in my wallet?"

Mitch and the others cracked up when the money was mentioned.

"You really don't remember anything, do you, Steve?"

"It's Stephen, and no."

Farah corrected him, "Stevie."

"Stevie, right. Shit, I don't know my correct name after last night."

"The groom gave it to you as part of the bet," Mitch continued.

"Bet, what bet," Stephen questioned, looking completely dumbfounded.

Please say the night ends there. Please say that I had to drink some shots or something and, for god sake's don't say that I-

"You got on the stage and stripped for everyone at the club! It was crazy! The only thing that you had on was your underwear, but you only kept that on so that the groom-to-be could shove fifties down your shorts!" One of the groomsmen burst out laughing and Farah chuckled a little at the idea, covering her mouth so as not to laugh more at the moment as it presented itself.

"No, I didn't!" Stephen didn't know how to feel. It was too late to take it back. And apparently, he was a pretty good dancer because he got paid nearly $500 bucks.

Farah confirmed it by doing a double take of his wallet when he took it out to show them how much he made that night.

"Damn, Stevie! That's a pretty good night's take in for your first time. You should come and work with me."

That's when Mitch's face nearly went white with surprise.

"What?"

The snow was still coming down around them, thick flakes floating down past their thick breaths that hung in the air. The joint had all but gone out now and everyone was beginning to get cold. They could also see the driver walking back to the bus and knew that the bus would be leaving shortly after that.

"You mean **you're** a stripper, Farah?" Mitch nearly stumbled in the snow when Stephen's friend nodded and opened her coat for all to see the stripper attire she still had on from the night before. The entire group began high-fiving Stephen and even tried to put him up on their shoulders. But the driver's voice cut through the cold and their mini-celebration.

"Time to board, ladies and gentlemen! Let's go. We leave in two minutes!" The driver climbed up the steps and back onto the bus, half-closing the hydraulic doors to keep the draft and the snow out.

The rest of the stragglers got on the bus shortly before it left. Stephen looked out the window at the Christmas decorations that lit the small plaza. Not far from him, Mitch and his friends cheered at Steve's conquests and Farah looked over at him and smiled, leaning into the comfort of him and his winter coat, the gorgeous woman falling asleep next to him as soon as the bus got onto the Interstate minutes later.

Is this what my Christmas is to look like; drunken nights I can't remember, bachelor parties, fucking strippers, earning money as a male stripper, all the while going under the aliases of Steve and Stevie?

When Stephen thought of it like that, it didn't sound so bad.

Things could be worse, Stephen thought to himself, soon drifting off as well to the lull of the bus as it passed over snow-covered roads, nothing in sight for miles with the exception of a few passing cars and diesel trucks.

Yes, Stephen, it could be worse. A lot worse.

CHAPTER FIVE
‑ "Do you see what I see?" ‑

When the bus finally pulled up to the station, several hours later, Stephen was still asleep. Farah had woken up and began putting her things away in the small purse she carried that she had stored underneath the seat in front of her. She shook Stephen lightly.

"Stevie, I think we're here."

Mitch nodded in agreement.

"Yeah, this is the main stop before the next three transfers for us. We'll be heading out here." He tapped Stephen on the shoulder, holding out his hand to him.

"Yeah, this is our stop, too." Stephen took Mitch's hand, still half asleep. Mitch shook it soundly, nearly waking Stephen up with the strong grip he had on him.

"Damn, you're the man, Steve! You made the bachelor party go to new heights, my friend! Let me know if I can do anything for you. I'd love to have you at my bachelor party if and when I get married. And you can bring your pretty friend here, too, if you like." Mitch patted Stephen on the shoulder and the rest of the groomsmen gave a quick salute as they grabbed their things from the overheard storage, filing off the bus to their next transfer.

"Well, that was rather weird!" Stephen noted, lifting himself up from his seat so Farah could get out. Stephen shook his head, trying his best to wake fully.

"Actually, I thought that was kind of cool. Doesn't make you as epic as you thought; you only slept with one stripper that night. I guess you'll have to settle for me and your stripper moves on the dance pole to keep your rep going."

"I think I can deal with that." He looked at Farah's perfectly round ass as it curved to the contours of her stripper outfit. She reached above the overheard and grabbed her winter coat to put it on.

"Stevie, did I just catch you looking at my goods?"

Stevie nodded.

"Well, we're going to have to do something about that now, aren't we?"

Stevie nodded again. He could feel the stirring of naughtiness begin to take hold properly, as it should after a story and a night like that.

He smiled at her. "I'm sure I can think of something. All this talk about strippers and poles and clothes off has got me thinking about a very specific pole."

Stevie reached out and grabbed Farah by the hips, pressing his newly acquired erection into her backside, her coat covering any naughtiness from the bus driver who had just gotten off the bus to unload the luggage from the undercarriage.

"Are you saying you want me to dance on this pole of yours, Stevie? Like I did last night?"

"You're going to have to refresh my memory, Farah."

"With pleasure." Her lips and hot breath met Stevie's, her hips still in his hands, her ass still pressing against his rigid member in anticipation of a rematch of sorts from the night before.

I won't let myself forget about the encounter with Farah this time, Stevie promised himself, feeling the curve of Farah's ass entrap his erection completely. Farah pressed herself hard against him.

"Where's your ride at, Stevie? I think we need to get out of here before we soil this bus."

Stevie had subsided for the moment. Stephen took a deep breath and let go of Farah's hips, looking out of the bus's windows for one of his older brothers. After all, they said they would pick him up. But, what he saw instead standing there near one of the bus terminals nearly put him into cardiac arrest.

Standing next to the car they had had sex in a number of times, Angela looked from passenger to passenger as each got off the bus, a look of excitement on her face as she watched the bus empty itself out into the show; another, then another, then another.

Stephen just stood, frozen in place on the bus.

"You have got to be fucking kidding me!" It was more of a whisper to himself, a warning of what might possibly happen but, when Farah heard it, she turned to him and followed his gaze.

"Is that her? Is that Angela?"

Stephen nodded his head, still in disbelief.

There, out by her beat up old, silver Honda Accord, half-covered in snow and waiting for him, was his ex-girlfriend, the real Angela, looking sweet and dainty, with a big Christmas present wrapped in her hands.

Her light blond hair was bundled up in a winter cap and she wore a thick scarf that hid those beautifully thin yet red lips. Her small frame was bundled up quite well for the winter season and, though Stephen couldn't see any of her skin with the exception of her face, the entirety of himself burned at the thought of touching her, holding her, being inside of her. His desire for her had not waned. It wasn't until Farah nudged him that he noticed again the present in his ex's hands and what her intent was.

And I bet it's just for me, too! Something to smooth over the rough edges of last night's discussion. Just the kind of chicken-shit thing she would do!

In another few moments, Farah had Stephen coming back to his senses.

"Well, what are you going to do?"

"I've got a plan. Can you just follow my lead?"

"I've come this far, haven't I? I think I can go a little further; just for the holidays. What did you have in mind?"

The little spark of naughty Stephen had seen earlier in her eyes came out then. Soon, Stevie smiled back out at her.

The bus driver had already left the bus to check-in with the bus depot when Stevie and Farah found a comfortable spot to enact Stephen's plan. No longer would Stephen be a victim to the break-up or allow his ex-girlfriend to wiggle her way back into his life with an apology, a gift, and some Christmas pussy. Stevie was going to go out with guns blazing.

As it should have been, Stevie reminded himself, pressing Farah against one of the bus seats facing Angela, peeling down the stripper's panties while he unzipped his pants shortly after, his rigid member alert and at the ready. It was almost as if his penis had overheard the plans to get back at the ex and sided with the idea altogether, pressing itself quickly into Farah, her ass urging, her hips wiggling him the rest of the way inside.

"Oh, fuck, Stevie! I'm beginning to like your plan more and more!" Farah draped her winter coat over the bus seat and laid against it, letting Stevie do the rest from behind, her hips in his hands once his cock was nice and wet from her own excitement.

"Just wait, Farah. You'll really like the ending!" Stevie's desire for the stripper had finally taken over. The sex and the blowjob that morning had only given him a taste of what she could do for him, but merely whet his appetite. Stevie smiled when she began to moan, Farah's hands grabbing at the seat in front of her the best she could as he drilled away, the bus slightly shaking with his thrusts.

"Shit, Stevie, that feels good! Don't stop! You got me right where you want me! You got this, alright!"

The shaking bus got Angela's attention, just as Stephen had planned. Wiping away the light layer of snow that had landed on her winter cap, she looked up at the bus through the snow coming down, Farah's hands pressed against the glass, bracing for each thrust that Stevie slammed into her. Farah's winter coat had fallen to the floor amidst a hard thrust and the stripper's breasts rocked back and forth, nearly touching the window, Farah now on her knees, taking up two seats. She smiled at Angela. And that's when Angela noticed who was fucking this gorgeous beauty from behind.

Stephen, loyal boyfriend of nearly a year, carrier of the accursed purse at so many functions and parties, the man who never lost his temper at her and always made her a plate of food first, holder of the door like a knight of old, and who was spirited enough to go down on her even when her last few boyfriends had no part in wanting to ever give her a new experience! Yes, that was he. And he was fucking the shit out of this woman.

And the woman loved it. Every sick, perverted, wet, and dripping inch that Stevie could give her, this woman took with a naughty smile. Every so often, Stevie even smacked her ass and told her something, his voice loud and angry. And the woman's paced quickened and met his.

Angela had never seen this part of Stephen before. And at the sudden sight of it, no matter how revolting it was to be happening in public, turned her on to no end. Angela even found that her panties were beginning to moisten from her own excitement.

She smiled at Stephen and hoped that, through the window, even with the snowy evening, he would see. And he did. And, though he was still thrusting into this woman, he smiled back. The moistness increased in between Angela's legs, a strong throbbing that desired attention. She wanted to drop the gift then and reach down to confirm that the desire was real; that her boyfriend of nearly a year had just turned her on by fucking another woman in front of her.

That's when Stephen climaxed and called out this woman's name. Though it was muffled, Angela could hear the desire and the lustiness in his voice.

It was deeper now, more baritone than it had ever been before. This woman had done something to him, changed him in some way.

Angela looked down for a moment, nearly in shame at seeing Stephen come and not having been a part of it.

I've been holding this beast at bay this whole time. I never let him be himself or do what he wanted to me. From the looks of it, it seemed to be fucking pleasurable as hell, Angela thought to herself, looking back up at the two of them on the bus. The bus had stopped rocking.

"Probably gotten what they wanted now", Angela remarked to herself, her hands sweaty around the sides of the box she held, shifting her feet in the snow to subside the throbbing between her legs. She was quite cold outside, but there were parts of her that were on fire and refused to be put out. She looked up and, just as quickly as the desirous feeling had come, it was gone. Both of them were smiling at her, that post-coital half-smile, looking directly at her. And Stephen held out one of his middle fingers at her. He mouthed the words 'fuck you' and it was as clear as crystal to Angela then, who dropped the gift in the snow as she watched Stephen and his new Angela climb down off the bus and walk by her without even a second look.

Yes, Steve's Christmas was the best he'd had in years. And so was Farah's for that matter.

The End

 Blowjobs for Everyone!

Written by Titus Strong

Chapter One
- "'Tis the season..." -

Donald McTaggert never knew what it was like to get a good blowjob. Many of them that he had been given were usually given under great duress or when a chick was "prepping" him for the actual ball game. This young man of a modest twenty-nine years had celebrated the fact that he got them at least, though he knew that they were more of a survival blowjob than anything else.

I want the real thing! I want the sexy look in a woman's eyes as she crawls up between my legs, completely intent on pleasing me and me alone, he thought to himself, picturing the scene in his mind, though he felt, deep down inside, that this would never happen. After all, much of what he called his present-day life had been the result of not getting what he wanted.

The shitty apartment in a shitty neighborhood, the shitty college loans that seemed to pile up faster than I can pay, and even the job.

Donald knew that he wasn't made for this place. He looked around at all the others sitting in the meeting room for the regular holiday mall speech given by none other than Mr. Douche himself, Jimmy Sloan. The sixty-something mall owner had been on his last legs for the last few years, covered with liver spots and coughing in between each couple of words he spattered out, though his will to live centered around making other people's lives around him completely miserable.

And it was not at the most opportune of moments.

In fact, the mall owner stared through the haze of others in the meeting room, all the managers for the regular season as well as the holiday season cramped inside of a room that held thirty-five but was forced with nearly seventy individuals, all tightly-packed and very few of them wearing deodorant.

The old mall owner spoke.

"Ladies and gentlemen, we have a problem. More than anything, we have a crisis on our hands!" He had to say the whole thing twice for the people in the back to hear, coughing up another lung that made him clutch a mall manager's shoulder in front of him uncomfortably.

"Our Mall Santa of seventeen years, Gerald Summers, has left us." Many employees oohed and aahhed, most even bowing their heads in prayer. But the old fart waved their concern away with a wrinkly hand.

"No, you dumbasses! He quit after his contract was up and went to the new mall nearly 20 miles away! He got offered a better price for his yearly Santa." The old man whispered under his breath. "Damn old man was killing me every year, practically getting a yearly salary for only a month and a half of work." Only Donald and a few others heard this last part though.

"We're in search of a replacement just for this Christmas Season. From November 2nd to December 31st, we need someone who can work days, nights, and weekends. They pretty much have to live here. And we need a manager to spot this Mall Santa the entire time so he doesn't leave before the holiday season which, as you well know, can get pretty fucking rough pretty quick!"

There were no bones about it. Christmas was a rough season, especially for mall managers. The security was amped up and, once Thanksgiving came and Black Friday followed, it was a mad house.

But who could out-Santa Gerald Summers, the happy-go-lucky Kris Kringle that kept children and parents coming back over and over again, year after year?

*   *   *

Tommy Reardon was not a Mall Santa nor did he ever hope to become one, even when he became old and flatulent. He hoped that he would be dead before either one of those things happened to him.　Rock-hard pectorals and chiseled abdominals were not something everyone could attain and he would be damned if he would waste them waiting to getting old. He shook the can of whipped cream in his hands and sprayed it across his half-naked body, covering the well-oiled parts first to see if the ladies around him took a liking.

Soon, the women that had been standing around his stage stood up, Tommy's strong hands pressing their faces into his muscular frame, forcing their tongues and lips to do things that they wanted to do anyway yet didn't have the courage to in front of a crowd.

That's okay, ladies, that's what I'm here for!

Tommy pressed his thick member that was nearly ready to burst from the bikini underwear he wore against one of the ladies around him and he felt her hands reaching up and around his thighs in excitement. The desperation in the blondes' eyes was terrifying to him. In each set of eyes out in front of him was a sea of want and desire that very few could offer out there in the real world, just outside the doors of *The Wet Seal*, the establishment that Tommy and many others had worked at since it opened four years ago.

In moments, a few soccer moms from the back as well as a cougar or two were approaching the front of the all-male strip club, holding five, ten, and twenty-dollar bills in their hands out to him willingly. Even a small group of bachelorette party girls were pushing through the crowd, their cheap $4.00 plastic princess tiaras hanging off the side of their heads in drunken defeat. They urged the bachelorette up front, pushing through the crowd of oglers to get her on the stage.

The bachelorette was a small, petite twenty-something that was in awe that there were such men in the world readily available and at her disposal as Tommy was at that moment. She was not nearly as drunk as her girlfriends, who seemed to be drunk only for the sheer fact that their cuter, more restrained friend was able to hook a man and they weren't. Tommy, a.k.a. "Slick Rick", knew this crowd all too well. And, as his strong arms lifted the bachelorette up onto the stage, Slick Rick knew her better than most men she had been with...or he would soon enough.

"Fuck me, Rick! Oh god, that feels so fucking good!" Tommy's alias always got more pussy that he did. Slick Rick leaned into the bride-to-be, grabbing for her curvy breasts as he drilled her from behind. It wasn't a gracious moment or one of his best moments, Tommy freely admitted, but he enjoyed his job and the benefits that it had given him since working here. Back in his dressing room, which consisted of a simple square room that held a wall mirror, a twin bed, and some chairs and costumes hanging on a metal rack, the bachelorette got everything that her eyes had wanted when she had been out on the stage minutes earlier.

"This is the special treatment your friends paid for," he said, in between his own moans of pleasure, his hands planted firmly on her hips as she held onto the side of the bed and side table in front of the wall mirror. Tommy watched it all. He enjoyed the thrill of seeing it from beginning to glorious end.

First, he had been cheered offstage and into the throng of women at the stage and, after several gropings by unseen hands, with his balls nearly mashed in a matter of obvious urgency by a desperate hand, he made it over to the bar and got a drink from the bartender. Patrick the bartender smiled at him and nodded over to the bachelorette party that had followed Tommy without him knowing, the bachelorette in tow just behind them reluctantly.

"We want you to give our friend a good last night out!" Tommy could barely hear the young woman over the next song coming on, though he knew what she was asking. In fact, all he had to do was look at the bride-to-be, who shied away from his gaze whenever he tried to make eye contact, to know what they all wanted.

They want me to fuck this bachelorette on her last night of freedom.

And, for Tommy, there was nothing more freeing that watching a soon-to-be newlywed down on her knees, her mouth full of Slick Rick's dick, clawing at his muscular thighs as his bikini underwear dropped down to his ankles so she could take the rest of him into her mouth.

All of this, of course, he watched from the great wall mirror, admiring not just the act, but himself as well. The bachelorette was just part of the decoration that filled his thoughts, something that kept him going on the stage nights after she was gone and married to whatever dim-witted guy would have her.

It wasn't just her; the bachelorette was just one of the many women that he had brought back into his private dressing room for a moment of pleasure and fantasy.

Slick Rick came back to his senses when the bachelorette climaxed on his cock, the muscles within her contracting, her form leaning over, shaking uneasily. She grabbed for the wooden bedpost and Slick Rick squeezed her hips, pressing deeper into her. She moaned slightly but, for Slick Rick, that wasn't enough. He wanted her slipping in and out of consciousness if at all possible. And, with Tommy Reardon's rock-hard dick and stamina of a bull, it was entirely possible. The petite bachelorette braced for impact as the stripper drilled her, the plastic crown atop her shaking head falling off and hitting the floor beneath both of their panting bodies.

Chapter Two
- "...TO GET YOUR JOLLIES!" -

Donald McTaggert never liked to displease anyone, no matter how much they treated him like a piece of shit. So, when the local mall owner came to him early-November and informed him that the Mall Santa they had on contract for the last 17 years had turned to the dark side (which was what the owner had deemed the newer, more upscale mall 19.7 miles away from them), Donald could do nothing but open his mouth to take charge of the near-impossible situation.

"Well, I can find a replacement. I know a few places that might have what we're looking for."

In reality, Donald knew no one. He knew nothing about the world outside of the mall for the last few years while being a manager with the exception of the Dunkin Donuts where he got his breakfast every morning and the interior of his own apartment, which was where he spent the remainder of his nights after getting off late from work every night.

Of course, there were exceptions for Donald. He had been laid recently, which was something that he could tell his guy friends about, if he had any guy friends.

It wasn't even that good to tell the truth, he reminded himself, allowing a little bit of the self-pity he felt leak out inside his head, much like the puddles on the inside of a leaky boat; not so much a threat but definitely quite annoying.

It wasn't that Donald was unattractive, which he wasn't. He wasn't by any means a hunk or a heartthrob either, but he could be considered a keeper or a catch compared to many of the carnival freaks that worked at the mall. He was in shape and sported a new cut from Great Clips every few weeks. He would never let allow his hair touch his ears and was somewhat conservative in his attire outside of work.

He was, as some people had called it, overly groomed. Not a metro sexual by any means, but he kept an ongoing set of khaki pants in his closet and stayed away from the newer fashion trends like they were the plague. Donald kept his fingernails and toe nails short and shared no joy of having facial hair at all, keeping his chin and jaw line free of facial "debris".

If there was anything that Donald was guilty of, it was of him not conforming to societal standards; he left that to the cretins and simple-minded folks. Those in the manager's meeting room with him now were what he tried to stay away from, but they were surrounding him; more and more of them, year after year.

It was as if a plague of stupidity had come and just decided to stay for a while. Indeed, it had gotten comfortable in Maple Pines Mall, just south of Minneapolis. Apple Commons was a quiet enough community, Donald knew that well; he had lived here all of his life.

However, he didn't know if it was something in the water or there was inbreeding going on, but all that decided to stay in the small town had very little sense. And he knew he wasn't an exception. For most of his youth he wasn't an exception. That's why he had left and gone to college, only to return to a dead-end job here in Apple Commons. However, he appeared cursed to walk the very same mall that he walked as a teenager.

He needed to do something, that much he knew. He just had no idea what to do. Around in a small town, there was no way to make your mark on the world unless you just started your own business and it took off. But there were only a few businesses that had taken off since he had come and gone from college.

Bif's Bait and Tackle Shop and Joan's One-Hour Dry Cleaners was not the type of mark that I wanted to leave, Donald thought to himself, though those were the two best examples that he had in Apple Commons. But, if you had told him that, in just one month's time, he would be pimping out another man to keep his job, he would have told you to go fuck yourself. But that was just what was about to happen.

The manager's meeting room was nothing more than the back-stock room to a Big Salez; a simply put rip-off to Big Lots that was attached to their mall and had replaced a shitty furniture store that closed some years ago. After Big Salez took an interest in the space, one of the deals of taking the space was made for them to share the space with the full managerial staff and allow meetings to take place in the back space that had been provided for their inventory receiving.

After throwing in a couple of shitty desks from the closed-down furniture store and a water cooler in the area, presto chango; the manager's meeting room was complete. However, the water cooler was just there for looks; it hadn't had working water in it since the furniture store was open.

For a world jumping into the technological age, the mall itself was barren as hell of it. With the exception of some of the shops in the mall using the Belly app and Starbucks being the only place to have Wi-Fi capability, there was no place for the assistant manager to begin his search for the new replacement.

So, he ended up having to get his laptop out of his car during his lunch break and sit in the Starbucks, searching his best for actors to play Santa. After a few times of going into other malls seeing the fake Santas strategically placed just outside the food court, he knew that he couldn't get just some schmuck to replace the irreplaceable, the great, the fabled Gerald Summers of so many years. He needed someone special.

That's when Donald's eyes spied **All Season Santa** on Google. He had checked a few places for a Santa actor but hadn't found anything that would work the schedule that they were asking; long hours, seven days a week, meet and greet, and even breakfasts with some of the kiddies on the weekends that were part of an organization that partnered with the mall.

He called the number shown on the site. A cute, female voice picked up on the other end.

"All Season Santa, this is Susan speaking, how may I help you?"

"Yes, my name is Donald McTaggert and I'm interested in a full-time Santa Claus for the holidays."

I hope this place works.

*   *   *

"They want what?" Tommy Reardon was still sore from the night before with the bachelorette. Not only did she leave satisfied, but she also took a few business cards with her for her friends. Tommy planted his shod foot up on the secretary's desk and stretched out a sore thigh muscle. She looked at him with disdain.

But there was a hint of desire there, too, Tommy noticed, his shirt half hanging off his muscled shoulders, the front open completely to show the complete package. He could still feel the dried-up sex juices on him, plastering his pubic hairs up against his thighs and clumping small sections together just above his penis, causing him to wince in pain a little bit in front of Lonna.

"Get in a bit too deep last night, Rick?"

He shot her his winning smile as he stretched himself out the rest of the way.

"You could say that." But he got back to the issue, pointing at the paper he had given her. It was a job request. "So, there's a mall that wants a Santa for the holiday season? Why are they calling here?"

"It was a transfer call from Susan, over at All Season Santa. I used to work over there before I started here. She says some mall is desperate to find someone as a replacement. Something about their regular Santa leaving or something like that."

"I'm not doing it! I quit all that holiday shit after what happened last time."

"For crying out loud, Tommy! It was just one time!"

"They wanted to stick a dildo up my ass, Lonna?"

Lonna didn't blush when he said the word dildo out loud; but she did begin to blush when she reminded him, "You didn't hear me complaining on my birthday when you did that for me."

"That was because it was your birthday." Tommy suddenly remembered Lonna's mouth and its abilities, her surprised face when he entered her. She was surprised mostly because everyone was there at her party that night.

'Rick, what are you doing?' And those moans of hers!

Slick Rick adjusted his impending erection so it wouldn't be so obvious and put his foot back down on the floor.

"And because you asked nicely. Besides, you know I'm not into that kind of thing, Lonna."

"I know, sweetie. I can guarantee you that this won't be anything like that. I only tasked you on this first because you said you wanted any extra work that came up and you used to act all those years ago."

"And I appreciate that, I do. It still means you're thinking about me. And you know how hard that shit makes me, Lonna."

The twenty-something let the flush in her face take over; fill in her cheeks and lips, her doe-like eyes looking back out at him.

Yeah, she's mine whenever I want her. Too bad she's got a boyfriend. I'd keep her as a regular if she didn't have to go home to him every night.

But such was the ways of lonely Tommy Reardon, sentenced to a life of back-to-back sex-capades and a plethora of titties that he could only fathom in his wildest of dreams.

He just needed an escape; an out. He had been planning on leaving the state and going West, moving to California, where his male attributes would be better suited; more of the world than just this poor, little town and its restless wives and sex-addicted cougars. Of course, Slick Rick had nothing against any of this; he saw what he saw: endless free pussy, a comfortable place to stay, a place to party, as well as a hefty pay to keep Tommy from having to work a part-time job.

What more could a man ask for?

Then he looked at the pay rate for the Mall Santa position on the paper. His erection got harder.

"Where is this place at again?"

Chapter Three
-"Fa- la- la- la-la- tio..." -

Marcy Leesman wasn't the best Donald had ever had, nor would she be the last; but she wasn't afraid of the male member. She gobbled it up like a champ. Donald had been given some pretty unacceptable blowjobs at one time or another, but the one that Marcy was giving him right now was exactly what he needed, especially after an extremely stressful day at work.

This is how it worked at Donald's residence when Marcy would arrive: They would say hi and give each other a three-second hug. Once that occurred, he would invite her in and take her coat. Donald would offer her something to drink, which she would either accept or decline. Once that occurred, he would invite her to sit on the sofa and watch some television while they talked about how their day went. All of this would take 20-30 minutes, more or less, with both of them knowing where it would end up; blowjob and a long, drawn out fingering. It wasn't exactly Netflix and Chill, but at least it was something.

Some of you may throw that off as pretty pathetic or, even worse, settling for the minimum, but Donald liked to think of it as the dues he had to pay for his monthly blowjob.

Some guys have girlfriends that don't even give it to them that much! Hell, some married men don't even get it at all!

All of this was true, Donald knew; but deep down, somewhere inside Donald, waited the person that wanted more. He didn't know how much more, so he couldn't tell Marcy or any other woman he would take interest in anything of that nature. To show interest would be to accept the possible fate of being with someone that you weren't really interested in. So, he was stuck in a rut, so to speak. But he didn't let that bother his monthly blowjob from Marcy.

Marcy's head popped up for a moment, her reassuring hand on his cock letting him know she was going to finish.

"Let me know when you're about to, Donnie!" He looked down at her for a moment, taking his eyes away from the muted television for a second. She seemed a little out of breath and, just around her lips, was a little red from sucking hard on his cock.

"Oh, I'll be sure to let you know, Marce!"

Their pet names were not cute or fuzzy or denoted any term of endearment, but were simply used as a way not to have to say each other's whole name, which had been the custom ever since they had first had sex, which had been nearly six months ago.

Now this is where Donald seemed to grow weary. He liked having sex, especially when another person was involved, and Marcy had given him that chance at her place one night when they came back from a movie.

But it was quick! Not one of my best moments!

Donald knew that every man had those moments; where the load wanted to come out almost upon inception at the enticing moment laid before them, and he wasn't an exception to this rule. It had happened to him twice; once with Marcy and once with an old ex-girlfriend April, a moment she took away with pride, attributing it to her "sensational" ability in the bedroom.

It was a moment, that was all. But Donald knew that many people, no matter how open-minded they said they were, based forever on a single moment. Marcy was no exception. Donald had no choice but to live in those moments; the ones that made him feel like a loser.

I can't get out of them!

Just then, Marcy's mouth rubbed against a spot on his cock that sent him jolting forward, his hand moving down to her head to stop her.

"I'm com...I'm..." But that's all he could get out before he came in her mouth, his eyes closing in pleasure as his legs shook with delight.

Then Marcy was up, her head pulling away from Donald's cock, which released a few small drops of cum out onto his lap. Marcy grabbed the cup she was drinking from and spit out Donald's orgasm in it.

"You fucking asshole! I told you to tell me when you were going to come!" She sat the cup down on the coffee table and began buttoning her shirt back up, her breasts still exposed from their make out session.

"I'm sorry, Marce, I couldn't help it! I tried to say something to you but it felt so good!"

"That's what all men say right before they come and ruin a woman's life! I thought you were different!"

Donald could hear the disappointment in Marcy's voice as she grabbed her coat and slipped her boots on, closing the door behind her. And, once again, Donald was in the moment that he hated more than Christmastime in the mall.

Loneliness.

Even during a fucking blowjob, the moment sprang up. I hate you, loneliness.

He wiped himself off with a paper towel he got from the kitchen and went to bed, knowing that he needed it to prepare for another day at the mall.

*   *   *

Tommy Reardon had never been so satisfied in all his life. Next to him in bed, a sex-starved cougar slept, satiated and content for the moment. Her dark brown hair fell about him and, as he looked around, he realized that he wasn't at his place at all. He had slept over. This was against his rules completely.

He looked down under the covers at his cock and saw that it was still well wrapped. He had at least done his one iota of responsibility before drinking and fucking himself into oblivion.

And oblivion is where I seem to be, the well-defined stripper noted, taking a look around him at the nicely decorated room. The walls were painted and the entire room had been made to match the light brown of the four walls around him, several slivers of light breaking through the thick curtains on the far wall.

Tommy lifted himself up on his elbows and was greeted with a full view of the older woman, from the ankles all the way up past her gorgeous, round ass to her shoulders, which were still comparable to a college girl's; the thin, unwavering path of flesh between the shoulder blades that Tommy liked so much showing on her as well.

He took more pleasure in cougars than any type of woman he had ever had in his time as a stripper. Of course, he had gotten laid plenty of times before that and even had a few girlfriends for brief periods of time. But what he did at the strip club as well as what occurred after work bordered on plain good, old-fashioned idol worship.

The women there were aching for a piece of the dancers on stage, even if it was for a moment in the back room, a deep-throating in the bathroom stall until the stud blew their load, or a romp in a parked car outside, which was Tommy's favorite, having some little cutie bouncing up and down on his prick until she seized in absolute pleasure, their heavy breathing fogging up the windows completely.

But cougars, Tommy thought to himself, staring over at what's-her-name's delicious physique, *they're a world all their own.*

First of all, cougars didn't play games with what was on their mind or what they wanted. They could easily give you a look, it could be at your body or straight at your cock as it bulged out from the tight spandex underwear the club owner made the dancers wear, but there was no shame in what the ladies wanted.

And the stamina of older women!

They had their heyday and sowing oats decades earlier, which meant that they had grown accustomed to a cock inside them at this point. This made for a good challenge; Slick Rick had to work for every moan that escaped their lips. And cougars didn't ask for emotional security; they were already secure with themselves and the life they had carved out for themselves. They didn't need or want a relationship with a man.

Tommy loved his job, what it gave him access to, as well as what it did for his ego, which was ripping and raring to go today, for whatever may be on the agenda.

Then he remembered he had the job interview for that Santa position at the mall. He had no idea what he was supposed to do, but for the amount of money they were offering, he was willing to do pretty much anything for it.

Tommy picked his boxers up off the floor and slipped himself into them, being sure not to wake up the hot cougar that was out cold next to him. He didn't know if he (or his dick) could handle another rousing round of her this morning, especially if he wanted to get this job. He re-familiarized himself with the cougar's living area, grabbed a cup of orange juice from the fridge and a bagel from the bread cupboard in her rather ornate kitchen, and made his way outside to his car.

Well, Mall Santa job, here I come!

*   *   *

Never had a person hated his job so much as Donald did at this moment.

Especially during the Christmas season. If there was any assistant mall manager in the world that could hate the holidays more, Donald was the fucking Grinch of Christmas time at the mall at the present.

All the toys, toys, toys, and the noise, noise, noise!

The snotty-nosed little tantrum-throwers Whoville-like motherfuckers and the stuck-up parents and their unlimited credit, all the while hunting for the best bargains! Like they needed to save money anyway! Those fucking trust fund spend thrifts!

Bah, humbug!

This was never Donald's intention for Christmas, more so for the majority of his young adult years. He had wanted to have the college experience, join a fraternity and be fucking a steady sorority chick. But all that disappeared when he looked at his bank account all those years ago.

Even in his early twenties, he knew that he wouldn't be making a college trip anytime soon. His mother and father were both old and into their retirement by the time he graduated from high school, him being the wonderful "surprise" to them when he was born. All that he had to work with was his smarts and this small town he was in. Little did he know, until it was too late, that small town folk rarely get out of the small-town setting.

But I have no choices at this moment. He looked around at the small-town mall folk as they prepared for the morning. The main doors to the mall had already been opened, which allowed for each manager of the shops in the mall to come in and set up their tills and inventory their morning stock from the night before.

Donald's job was to unlock the doors, turn off the alarm to the mall, reset the mall security tapes from the night before, log in all occupants coming in, as well as monitor the senior citizens that mall-walked in the early morning hours. Once it began to get cold outside, the senior citizens would make their way to the malls in waves, sporting their workout attire and sour-faced grimace at everything that was living around them.

As they passed by Donald, he greeted them with a quick "Good morning", but their sour-puss visage cut through the assistant mall manager's bullshit greeting and they made their way into the mall.

Yeah, you too, you dried up, wrinkly old fucks! Go to a fucking gym! This is a mall. A Fucking Mall!

But the shitty salary kept Donald's comments at bay and he, instead, thought on the Mall Santa that was coming that morning, to sit in on a sample day at the mall. After all, it was the first weekend in November and it wouldn't be overly busy for kids.

Bring on the Mall Santa! Bah, motherfucking humbug!

Much to the displeasure of Donald McTaggert, Tommy Reardon was not an old man with a beard. Instead, he was pretty much a strip-o-gram with a cheap Santa Suit in a duffle bag.

"I'm sorry, but I think there was some kind of misunderstanding. You're not an old man." Donald looked apologetically at his applicant.

But Tommy didn't stir from his place at the shitty table at the back of Big Salez.

"Santa Claus doesn't have to be old!"

"Yes, actually, he does. And he needs a beard. A real one! All the kids that are losing their belief in Santa pull it to check to see if it's attached. If it comes off, there can be lawsuits! Believe me, I've seen it before!"

Tommy was dumbfounded. "Shit! I didn't know it was that serious. I just thought anyone could sit in the chair."

"I'm sorry, but this is not going to work out."

"Are you seriously paying the amount that my secretary told me?"

"Yeah, plus you get a portion of the proceeds from the photography set. Usually adds up to a thousand or two a week, just depends on how many customers you bring in."

"You're shitting me? What do old Santa Claus look-alikes do with all that cash, anyway?"

"That's usually all they have to work for the entire year."

"Holy shit! And nobody knows about this kind of cash?"

"What do you mean?"

Tommy smiled and Slick Rick came out in his smile.

"So, if I get this job, I can make the salary and a portion of the proceeds, all based on commission? And all I have to do is play Santa for 8 hours a day from now until New Years?"

"And your three weekend appearances with the Salvation Army, Goodwill, and the Children's shelter that is contracted. But," Donald looked back down at Tommy's application. "Mr. Reardon, I can't hire you. You're not old enough."

"What if I can make myself older?"

"How do you plan on making that happen?" Donald looked intrigued.

Two words: Judy Looms.

To Tommy Reardon, before he became his alter ego Slick Rick, Judy Looms was the lone wolf lady he ran with. She was a backstage hand that had a wonderful set of hands and an addiction to wearing Tommy's cock in a myriad of ways on her body. She wanted him everywhere, all at once. She took him in her mouth, kept her hands stroking him when he wasn't inside of her; fuck, they practically spent their time together in bed or fucking in different locations in her apartment loft not far from the local theater she volunteered for while she was working her way through college.

But she was also a make-up artist; and a damn good one. Tommy still had her number, though they had been on the outs for some time, ever since he took the job at The Wet Seal four years ago. He wondered if she would still answer. He stepped away from the table and from Donald and looked up her number in his call list, pressing the dial button on his cellphone.

She answered on the first ring.

"Well, if it isn't Tommy Reardon coming to call on me."

"Looms, sweetie, I need you here."

"Where's here? I hope you're in bed waiting for me, love, because I have this itch that only you can scratch!"

He told her the situation and she was only too eager to help. In another hour, she was there; make up kit and all, transforming him right before Donald, who was still staring at her beauty. Her body, her form, her personality, not to diminish her pouty lips and full breasts that practically urged themselves out of her sports bra she threw on at the last moment. She wore a flannel shirt over the sports bra and a beautiful winter coat when she had come in, but all of those things were discarded.

She kept her body as close to Tommy's as possible, many times letting her breasts rest on his shoulders or back whilst attaching his realistic beard with spirit gum.

She looked over at Donald as he watched her do her magic.

"You see, I was the make-up and set artist for my community theater's rendition of *A Christmas Carol* a year back. They wanted the Ghost of Christmas Present to resemble Father Christmas. These are pretty much the same facial prosthetics that I used."

When the make-up artist turned Tommy back around to show Donald, he looked better than their old Mall Santa could ever look. Tommy even had a perpetual smile plastered on his face using the prosthetics.

"Tommy, because you're going to be in front of a crowd for a longer duration than a theater showing, I took the liberty of adding a smile to your face for you so you won't get tired. After a few hours of smiling for cameras, you're face muscles will be useless. The forever smile will work wonders for the crowds."

This time, it was Donald's turn to be dumbfounded.

"Why doesn't anyone do this full-time?"

Judy looked at Donald with condescension.

"Most are still limited in imagination, scope, or understanding that Santa Claus is still one of the most revered parts for society today. Just by posting an old man in a suit on a throne for children to visit him doesn't make him Santa. He must act the part; he must **become** the role."

Judy sat in Santa's lap and laid a kiss on Tommy, who answered it back with a reassuring grope of her exquisite breasts, a simple sign that showed more would be offered to her at a later date.

Donald looked at the work she had done on his applicant and was still astounded that it was the same person. He pointed to the rest of Tommy's attire. After all, he didn't fit the Santa Suit that the mall provided, and it was one of the more realistic suits that had ever been made for a Mall Santa.

"What about his size? How is he going to pass as an old man and jolly old elf?"

Judy lifted her lithe form from Santa's lap and grabbed her bags that she had brought in from her car. She pulled out a fat suit and laid it on the table.

"The suit forms around its wearer and, as long as you have your skivvies on underneath, it shouldn't cause chaffing at all. There's a small air pump that's charged in the bag I'm going to leave that you can shoot through air to ventilate and keep the wearer from sweating profusely underneath during his breaks. There's also foot and body powder you can shoot into the suit that keeps any smells from beginning to form.

Donald smiled at Judy. Judy smiled at Tommy.

Tommy smiled at Donald. "So, when do I start?"

* * *

After Judy said her goodbyes to Tommy and left him to his future as a possible Mall Santa, Donald explained that it wasn't that easy of a fix.

"You see, I don't hire you based upon me just liking your look. The mall owner needs to do the final approval, and that's only after you sit as Santa for a day. You ready?"

"You mean today? Right now?"

Donald looked at his watch. It was 12:30. After interviewing Tommy, waiting for Judy to get here and watching the transformation for himself between putting out proverbial fires at the mall, Donald had already blown through two and a half hours of his shift. At 1:00 p.m., the Mall Santa area would be set up and ready for Santa Claus. The mall assistant manager had already walked by the set-up area once; there was a line of parents with their kids waiting for Santa Claus to arrive.

Motherfucking Christmas! Dammit, you people! Why can't you come another day?

The pressure was on for Donald McTaggert. Donald only wished he could catch a break; just once. The mall owner would be by to check his progress on the Mall Santa debacle.

Donald hoped beyond hope that this Tommy Reardon fellow would at least keep the owner off his back until he could find a full-time Mall Santa, if he even made it that far after today.

*   *   *

The moment Tommy Reardon sat down in Santa's chair, he was the thing of dreams. First, he smelled good. Apparently, Judy had given him something that made him smell absolutely fabulous to both children and the female population bringing their kids. Soon, the moms were on Santa's lap as well, taking pictures and smiling like little kids asking Santa for the bestest present of all. Santa would even stand up from time to time and walk around his workshop created as a set, waving to little children, to families doing their shopping, even taking selfies with some of the employees at their shops, handing out candy canes. With the appearance of this Santa Claus, the whole mall got into the spirit of Christmas.

It was as if Tommy Reardon was somehow the full embodiment of Christmas behind all that made up and Santa suit. After three hours, Santa took a quick break to cool off in the back and Donald was there to meet him. Donald opened up the flap in the back of the suit and put the air pump hose in, turning the small air pump on.

"You're doing fantastic, Tommy! I never expected this from you! The whole crowd loves you! Fuck that; the whole mall loves you!"

Donald couldn't tell if Tommy was really smiling underneath the Santa make up but he thought that he was when he answered.

"So, does that mean that I get the job?"

Donald quickly halted Tommy's thought on that subject with a wave of his hand.

"Remember, it's all up to Mr. Sloan in the end. He should be here any minute."

And, like clockwork, the dried-up old prune of a man showed, taking his waltz around Santa's workshop, tinkering with this thing, critiquing something else, a veritable douche of an old man, complete with misery and OCD rolled into one.

That's why Donald found it hard to believe it when the old man smiled at him and patted him on the back.

"Outstanding replacement, Donald! I was surprised at first, but then I started getting the feedback from the entire mall as I passed around. One day and Santa's already making the place brighter!"

Old man Jimmy Sloan eyeballed Tommy in his Santa outfit, trying to pick something out that could possibly be wrong. As Santa took his place back on the Santa chair, Mr. Sloan could already see the line waiting to sit and get their picture taken with Santa.

"Where did you get him from, McTaggert?"

Donald wasn't quick on the sly but he did his best.

"Let's just say it's my Secret Santa, Mr. Sloan."

Mr. Sloan clapped Donald on the back and moved along with his entourage of ass-kissers to the next part of the mall, content for the moment that the Mall Santa debacle had been subdued.

Not far from the front of the line, an attractive figure caught in Santa's eyesight. The blond wore a satisfyingly tight black skirt with a light blue blouse that clung around her ample bosom, low cut and showing enough cleavage to make a stripper choke.

"Oh shit, it's her!" Tommy mumbled under his beard, of course, making sure that there were no children or photographers around when he said this. He was just taking his seat at his Santa chair when he saw her. She was with two other women and their little rug rats, both of which Tommy Claus recognized immediately. Tommy kept his gaze directed at the photographers in front of him and the next little kid that came to sit in his lap and ask for shit.

"Merry Christmas, little boy! And what is it you want from Santa this year?" The little infant with a bowl cut just stared at Tommy Claus as if he were a disease; then broke into screams and cries of terror. His parents soon came to the rescue.

"Poor little guy. Looks like he wants his mommy and daddy." The photographer managed to get a few shots before the crocodile tears started. The parents left with a smile and a crying infant. Tommy Claus didn't have to smile due to the make-up, but he waved goodbye to them and welcomed the next child and their parents up.

A few people behind, the blond hottie in the tight black skirt and her two girlfriends moved closer. Tommy Claus did his best to keep his eyes on other things, hoping that she didn't see him or make him out through the make-up. He had no idea what she would do, or what they all would do, if they recognized Slick Rick from The Wet Seal, the all-male strip club that they all frequented together.

They came and they went through the line, never taking a second look back at Tommy Claus and his fantastic disguise. Tommy breathed a sigh of relief.

The day wore on.

Chapter Four

-"Follow me in merry measure..." -

The day was a success. Tommy nailed the part of Mall Santa with ease, signing for the job for the rest of the season, his salary for the rest of the year skyrocketing with this cakewalk of a job. Sure, he would have to cut it down at The Wet Seal and only work a few hours a week. But it would only be for a little while, until he finished his contract out here. Jimmy, the manager, would understand completely.

'Slide in where it's the wettest, Ricky my boy!' That was Jimmy's mantra he lived by. After Tommy's second week at The Wet Seal, he had been told this. And he had been given his name. Of course, that was a whole different story for another time.

Though it wasn't very hard work, he was exhausted on the first day. The only thing that he wanted to do was drive home, take a quick shower, and hop in bed. He made it out to the mall parking lot an hour before the mall closed, the buzz of the holidays thick in the air. He hefted the duffle bag with all of the make-up and prosthetics onto one shoulder as he made his way to his car.

"Hey there, Slick Rick!" Tommy lifted his head up, still in the process of opening the trunk and putting his bags in, when he caught sight of her again. This time, it was outside and he was half out of the Santa costume. The beard and facial prosthetics were gone, replaced by a clean-shaven Tommy Reardon who definitely wasn't ready to deal with this kind of thing. But he played it casual.

"Oh, hi, Lynette."

Lynette Tinkerman.

Her name was unforgettable. In fact, in all the times that they had fucked, he had been given instructions to call her by her first name and, as he came, to call her by 'Ms. Tinkerman', continuously slapping her ass until he was finished. Well, unless she had him tied up. Then, he was to shake helplessly in the leather straps that kept him bound and wait for her to devour him in every way possible. Indeed, she was one of the naughtier ones that Slick Rick had met.

If she wasn't one of the most delicious cougars that Tommy had ever met in his stint at The Wet Seal, he didn't know who was. This woman could take all of him in her mouth and ask for seconds as soon as he was done. There had been a great many women in Slick Rick's short existence, but this long-legged lady intimidated the hell out of him, making little Tommy Reardon almost shake in his snow boots as he stood there now.

Tommy played it as safe as possible outside the mall parking lot, not saying anything about the stage name she had just called him by.

"Didn't expect to see you here in this neck of the woods, especially with your clothes on!"

"Yeah, just doing some Christmas shopping." Tommy shoved the bag with the Santa suit down into the trunk haphazardly, slamming the trunk down so he could see Lynette as she approached. The parking lot was still pretty full but the hustle and bustle was all inside the mall and not outside in the parking lot. So Tommy was able to see clearly the way Lynette was looking at him as she sauntered up to his car.

"You know, Santa knows when you're lying, right? ...and so does Lynette!"

"What would I be lying about, Lynette?"

"Really, Rick? I saw you in that mall as Santa Claus. Shit, my niece sat her kid in your lap, for fuck's sake! In fact, a few of the women that I know that know you knew it was you, too. It was kind of hot. It turned us on to see Slick Rick all dolled up and incognito like that."

"That's great, Lynette. You know where you can find me."

"That's right, I do. Right here." She paused, moving closer. "It's even more convenient now because I don't live too far from here. Now I don't have to spend all that time and money driving out of town to see you."

A thought popped into Lynette's mind. You could tell this because of the way she shifted in her high heels and focused her eyes on Tommy the more she thought, taking a couple of seconds in between to consider something new; something naughty. The corners of her mouth broke into a sly smile.

"You know, we could always snuggle up by the fireplace and fuck like rabbits."

Immediately, Tommy's flaccid member came to attention in his pants. It wasn't every day that he was brought to a cougar's home, let alone to one of his favorites. But he had work tomorrow.

Early work tomorrow. Mall Santa kind of work. He knew Lynette was up for fucking all night and into the morning.

"That may not be the best idea, Lynette."

The blond-haired cougar looked around the mall parking lot and stepped closer to Tommy, looking him in his eyes.

"Well, we can just fuck right here then, if that's okay with you." She could see the idea of it processing in Tommy's eyes. She knew he liked the feel and the taste of her.

She would never be satisfied with just a taste. That's how she was. Always teasing, always taunting, always taking bits and pieces in her mouth, in her hands, making sure every part that could was dripping with anticipation at her next move.

Who the hell am I kidding, I want this just as much as she does!

In another moment, Lynette leaned herself back against his car and let Slick Rick take over, Rick grabbing a little handful of hair as he pressed his erection against her, unfastening the Santa belt from his waist.

"Is this what the bad auntie wants, huh?" She had prided herself on being a fantastic aunt; free of children herself, with nieces and nephews galore. But Lynette just wanted some naughty. And Slick Rick had no qualms about giving it to her.

He let the red Santa pants drop down around his black Santa boots and felt Lynette's cold hand wrap around his dick. Slick Rick jerked in response but it only turned him on more.

"No touching, auntie. You know you don't get to see your gift until Christmas. You don't want to be a bad girl, do you?"

Lynette simply purred in response, pulling her panty hose down and off quickly, lifting up her skirt so that she could get Rick's prick inside of her.

"I have so many answers for that, Santa. I want to be good but I know I can't have everything I want for Christmas. So, can I just have a taste?"

"A taste?" This meant so many things for Rick, who had more ideas than just sugarplums dancing in his head. His cock was rock hard and he was ready to pummel Little Miss Lynette within an inch of her attractive life.

"Can you come in my chimney, Santa Claus?"

*Oh, **that's** what she wants!*

Slick Rick wasted no time and, after pulling her back against the car with a small handful of hair, he entered her, immediately feeling her legs wrap around the backs of his thighs.

"Oh, Santa, I don't know if my chimney's big enough for you."

"We'll make it fit, little Lynette. Don't you worry, Santa will come tonight!"

Though Rick was somewhat tangled in his Santa pants, he was very limber and flexible; years of dancing on stage made him able to put himself into nearly impossible angles.

But I need a taste of her, Rick decided, pulling his rock-hard member from her glistening chimney. In a quick pump of his muscular arms, Lynette was no longer facing him directly but was looking down at him now, pressed high against his own car, his face buried between her legs, creating a jolt of immediate pleasure once he pushed his tongue deep into her moistness.

"Oh, fuck, Rick!"

She dropped the role-play pretty fast, Rick thought to himself, noting that Lynette was too overcome with pleasure to complicate her mind with names at the moment. Slick Rick had barely gotten into his routine with Lynette, of being naughty and receiving naughty in return, when he heard someone coming up to them from behind.

"Um, Santa. Can I speak to you for a minute?" It was Donald, his boss, and he had a small make-up kit in his hand that Tommy had apparently left on the counter in the back room.

Lynette urged him to continue.

"I'm almost there, Rick."

"Rick? I thought your name was..." Donald guffawed, but was interrupted by a nervous Tommy Reardon. He pulled his head out from between Lynette's legs, disappointing all parties involved, and pulled his Santa trousers back up from around his ankles, covering his own rigid, wet excitement from view. He let Lynette slide down the car the rest of the way and get firm ground beneath her still shaking legs.

"That's a stage name, Donald."

Lynette could tell that she wasn't going to be finished off anytime soon so she pulled her skirt down from the prying eyes of Slick Rick's new boss, composing herself the best she could.

"You know where I live, Ricky. We **will** finish this later." She pressed up against him as she left, running her fingers over the hard erection that throbbed for her under Santa's trousers.

"And it's very warm where I live, Ricky boy. Just you remember that."

Tommy zipped up his Santa pants as Lynette went to her car, the naughty Santa turning his attention back to the severely displeased face of Donald McTaggert.

This isn't going to go well.

CHAPTER FIVE

-"STRIKE THE HARP AND JOIN THE CHORUS" -

"So, let me get this straight; you're a male stripper who, not only dances for money, but fucks for it, too? And you're good-looking **AND** you have a big dick?"

The two of them sat in the Big Salez meeting room they had interviewed at earlier that day. No one was around. Only the cleaning crews were patrolling the building with their cleaning carts, coming in and out every so often to drop off full trash bags of garbage in the trash compactor on the other side of the meeting room.

"Yeah, I guess you could put it that way."

"You're fired!" Donald got up and began walking away. Tommy threw his hands up in response to protest, following him out of the meeting room and into an empty Big Salez show floor.

"I'm only officially hired today, how can you fire me?" Donald turned around and tapped on the clipboard in his hand.

"Easy. I just did it. See, it says right here, 'New Mall Santa fired. Replace with another Santa; one that doesn't strip and sell himself for money.'" Donald was writing it as he was saying it. It was on a scratch piece of paper from the list of toppings he had wanted on his sub for lunch. But, to him, it counted for something.

"Did I do something wrong?"

"No." Tommy could tell Donald was lying from his awful poker face.

"Did I say something to offend you?"

"Not that I can remember."

"Then what is it? What kind of an asshole are you anyway, to fire someone on their first day? Everybody loved me!"

At that comment, Donald stopped.

"I'll tell you the kind of asshole I am, what's your name again?"

"It's Tommy. Tommy Reardon."

"Fuck, your name is even cool! You know what, I'm just gonna come out and say it; I don't like your kind, Tommy!"

"What kind is that?"

"Do you see where we're at, Tommy?"

"In the mall?"

"Yes, a fucking mall!"

"What does that have to do with anything?"

"Do you know where you're at?"

"I don't really know. Google maps brought me here."

"This mall isn't even **on** the map! You're out in the middle of Bumfuck, Egypt, man! There's nothing here! This place doesn't really exist to the rest of the world. You come in and change all that; in one day you're able to do that? How?"

Tommy didn't know how to answer. On one hand, he didn't want to incriminate himself even further by telling Donald that what he had seen was just a little bit of foreplay, that the real games were to be had a little bit later that evening.

Actually, as soon as I leave from here, Tommy reminded himself, the member in between his legs still throbbing, reminding him that the finish line was nowhere to be had at the moment.

On the other, he didn't want to show Donald pity. Pity meant weakness to Tommy and, if there was anything that Tommy hated more than a cheap tipper at the strip club, it was weakness. Sure, timidity played a part in the game he had with many of his paying clients at the strip club where he worked, but wasn't that the role of the man; to dominate the woman in all shapes, forms, and fashion? For fuck's sake, males have the thrusting member for a reason!

But there was something else behind his boss's anger, something that seemed a bit extreme. After all, he was stuck here at the mall, day after day; he didn't seem to get out much and see a lot of people or meet new women.

After all, he did say that this place is in Bumfuck, Egypt. And what do men want more than anything else in the world? Well, the real men at least.

"Only thing I know is that I want this job. I was made to do it! And it could work out for the both of us!"

"How would it work out for the both of us? You seem like you're the one reaping the benefits from it. Your first night here and you're get laid in the parking lot!"

"I can help, Donald. I have more friends than just her."

Donald heard his name, heard the sincerity in Tommy's voice. And he could still picture that cougar's ass planted on the male stripper's car, legs hoisted up like something from Cirque du Soilel. He wanted that, that ease with women that Tommy had. But how would Tommy be able to get it for him.

"What kind of friends do you have?"

*   *   *

"No one has ever done anything this nice for me before, I just want you to know that." Tommy nodded in understanding as he led Donald back into the Big Salez shitty makeshift office and handed him a roll of paper towels, closing the door behind him.

Tommy could hear Donald's question through the door.

"What will I need this for," referring to the roll of paper towels.

"Oh, you'll see." One call. That was all that Tommy had to make to turn this situation around for the better; specifically, for his betterment.

Melinda May was her stage name. Tommy didn't know what her given name was and he thought she liked it better that way. He had met her at his first erotic convention when he first started at The Wet Seal. He had been paid for a full day's work just to attend the convention and stand at the booth in some tight boxer briefs that showed off his package, handing out discounted tickets for the boss's establishment. She had been across at another booth, signing autographs.

She was in the record books for sucking the most dicks in the shortest amount of time, a regular blowjob legend. It didn't take long until Tommy was over there, chatting it up with her. By the end of the day, Slick Rick had sampled her blowjob techniques and gave her a strong B+ all the way across the board.

She was another in his call list if he ever needed anything.

Her maroon Chrysler Sebring pulled up a little later, after all the doors were closed, after all in the mall had come and gone. Even the janitors were in another wing of the mall, so no one would disturb them. They wouldn't see her coming in or Donald letting her out some time later.

She smiled at Tommy when she saw him at the door, giving him a kiss on the cheek and a hug before moving further in the dimly lit mall.

"You're into some freaky stuff now since we last met, huh, Rickie?" She was covered from head to toe in a white snow bunny outfit that showed off her ample curves, in both the ass and thigh department. Her tits, however, were covered up well. You could only see mass, not form at the moment. But Tommy was sure that would change in a few minutes.

"Oh, you know, adding things to my repertoire lately. Don't want to feel under qualified or anything." He felt Melinda's warm, gloved hands on the package between his legs that was still slick with Lynette's anticipatory juices.

"Oh, Rickie boy, I've seen your resume and you've got quite the qualifications, alright." Her fingers stroked the outlines of his member as she moved her hand away, sending a strong jolt through Slick Rick's thighs, reminding him of what awaited him just a few miles away; a cougar that would launch herself into a fuck frenzy once he arrived.

"Thank you, Melinda. I take that as a compliment. However, the present situation at hand-"

They walked through the back hallway until they came to a divide that separated the mall and Big Salez sections. They made their way through to the Big Salez meeting room.

"You say this guy is your co-worker or something? You turn over a new leaf and start doing people favors now or what?"

Slick Rick thought of all the favors he had done in the last few years and Melinda was right; this wasn't his modus operandi at all. In fact, he could only name two or three favors that he had bestowed upon others where he hadn't expected something in return.

"You could say that, Melinda."

"I'm all about the season of giving, Rickie. But you know that already though, don't you?"

He turned to the porn star and smiled his regular "up-to-no-good" smile at her. She was a beauty; *but more of a statue in which to look at from a distance and not touch*, Slick Rick reminded himself, looking at the parts of her that were real as well as the parts that were added some time later when she had decided which world she wanted to live in. It was pretty much the same world that he had been living in for so long.

"Yes, indeed, I do. That's why I called you directly. You're the best I know."   They stopped at the Big Salez meeting room door. Slick Rick put his hand on the doorknob and leaned closer to her.

"If you do this for me and everything happens for me like I hope it will, I will owe you big time, Melinda May. You hear me?" He leaned in closer and rubbed his lips lightly on her left cheek, letting them graze her own lips. Melinda breathed him in deeply. It wasn't every day she got to have studs asking for favors, let alone one willing to return the favor in any way possible.

"And you do know that I will call in that favor, right? I won't leave you hanging, Rickie. You will be returning that favor, every inch of you will be."

Rick smiled. Melinda smiled. They were in agreement; now for the business.

"Don't go easy on him."

"When have you known me to do that?" She licked her thick lips, letting Rick open the door for her.

Donald nearly dropped his clipboard in response to seeing this fantastic specimen of a woman come through the door.

"I'm Donald." That was all he could manage out of his salivating mouth.

"I'm Melinda May." She took off her thick, winter coat and draped it over a nearby chair at the meeting room table, grabbing the zipper to her one-piece outfit. Her tanned breasts popped out of the top of the flight suit style outfit, her perk nipples responding to the chilly air in the meeting room.

"Wow, that was fast! Why don't we talk for a minute, you know, before-" Melinda was already getting to her knees. Donald felt her hard nipples rubbing against the inside of his thighs, his dick responding immediately to her movements.

And to her mouth. And to that smile. And to her intentions with her mouth and, most of all, to those titties.

She smiled at him, reaching for his work belt and the zipper of his work pants.

"Fine. You do the talking."

But he didn't know what to say. And that's when she devoured him in her mouth whole, in one quick motion.

"Holy fuck, that's nice!"

And it was in that moment that Donald McTaggert felt the hate inside him dissolve; the angry Bah-humbug attitude that he had harbored angst at the crowds, the inept customers, the corrupt salesmen soliciting just outside the mall to his incoming customers. All these things and a great many more ill-wills towards others were forgotten. The only thing he cared about at that moment was watching Melinda May's head bob up and down, keeping time with his jerking legs, his hands going for her hair but not wanting to upset her rhythm that she had perfected over the years. He grabbed at the meeting table just behind him and braced for what, he knew now and would know forever, was the best blowjob of his life.

Donald soon found out why he was given the paper towels.

CHAPTER SIX
- "SING WE JOYOUS, ALL TOGETHER" -

"Blowjobs for everyone!" The crowd at the local dive bar down the street from the mall looked at Donald like he was crazy. Nevertheless, he didn't give a fuck because he was drunk. And all the thanks went to, yet again, Tommy Reardon for making it all possible. He raised his glass high and Tommy met it in mid-air, letting the two glasses clink together.

"I really don't know how to thank you." Tommy nodded his understanding and held up his empty bottle of IPA at the bartender that walked by, another one coming up for him shortly after.

"It's fine, Donald. I understand you a little bit better now. I kinda know why you were so pissed at me earlier in the parking lot."

The mall manager looked at him with glazed eyes and a lucid stare.

"You do? Really?" And a drunken slur.

"Yeah, I do." He waved his IPA at everyone in the bar. The stud continued.

"I don't know how to relate to regular life. I've never really been good at it. I started acting in school because I could escape all the real shit and live in a fantasy world. When I started stripping, it only furthered the fantasy world. I got what I wanted when I wanted it. And whomever I wanted. There was no doubt, no temptation that I could not overcome. I never really lived. I just... experienced things."

"Wow, that's pretty deep for a stirper. I mean strip... stripper."

"A stirper? Wow, you're really drunk, Donald."

"Do you have any idea how good that blowjob was, Tommy?"

"I can imagine."

"I'm sure you can. You've probably had like 10 just this week. And that woman out in the parking lot - Holy shit was she hot!"

Oh shit, Lynette! I almost forgot about her! He looked at the drunken Donald McTaggert and slapped a twenty down on the bar for the bartender and finished what he could of his IPA before moving away from his seat next to his drunken manager.

"Can you call this guy an Uber? He doesn't need to be driving tonight."

"Sure thing, pal." The bartender reined in the last of the drinks in front of Donald without him knowing because he was still sitting at the bar, clueless as to why his new friend had left all of a sudden.

"Was it something I said?" But his words were lost on the air because Tommy Reardon was already out the door and in his car.

Three missed texts and two missed phone calls later, Slick Rick made it to Lynette's place, hoping beyond hope that he hadn't kept her waiting too long and made her get another living energizer bunny for her late-night play.

The front door had been left unlocked. He walked in and past the grand foyer and the living room and to his appointed destination. All of the lights were out except for the stairwell backlighting, leading him up to the second-floor master bedroom, where she had played many games with him in the past, sometimes even spending the weekend in the room, twisting and turning beneath the covers, fucking each other until the other was bruised and raw.

Then he saw the bedroom door open as well. It was cracked only a hair and a small sliver of light was coming from it.

For him, he had no way to tell; well, not until he walked in and saw Lynette under the sheets with someone else.

"I'm too late, huh? It's totally my fault."

He could see Lynette's ass high in the air at the edge of the bed, her torso and head covered by the sheets. Her head was thrashing about between the other person's legs. The other person let out a squeal of pleasure.

Squeal, Slick Rick thought, grabbing the covers up for himself. In one quick tug, he unveiled the other party - and was surprised to see another woman receiving oral from Lynette. The sexy cougar turned around and wiped her mouth against the other woman's inner thigh, smiling at Slick Rick.

"You're never too late. But it is *your* fault. I had to bring Nancy over for a few drinks to settle me down and, well, I think you know the rest. Say hi, Nancy." Nancy shook a foot at Rick and lifted her head up to give a quick seductive smile. He recognized her from The Wet Seal almost immediately. She had come to the club with Lynette a few times before. And she was a cougar as well.

Lynette continued. "And I figured it's Christmas time and you've given so much to us, Slick Rick. I figured we'd give a little bit back. You game?"

"What are you talking about, Lynette? Am I game? I'm motherfucking Slick Rick!" He slipped his shoes off and did away with the Santa trousers in one flick of his leg, sending them spiraling out into the darkness beyond the bedful of cougars.

"The question is, are you game, Lynette?"

"I guess we're about to find out, aren't we?" Lynette turned herself over and, in one fluid movement, found Slick Rick upon her, pressing into her, finding the spot he had started on in the parking lot with his tongue. She let out a slight moan of pleasure.

"Yes, Lynette, we are!" After getting a proper taste of her on his lips, the only man in the room used his festively rock-hard member against her. Slick Rick felt his throbbing member inside of Lynette come alive with a renewed vigor for unfinished business. Then he felt Nancy's hands on him as well, pulling his face up to her still-heaving breasts for some attention. He met one of her nipples with just as much zest as he could whilst drilling Lynette the way she needed it.

Nancy's dark hair draped down over her shoulders as she came for him then, her fingers deep inside of her own yuletide box, tired of watching the fun being had without tasting a bit of it herself.

"My turn, Lynette. I want to feel him now."

"Then you get it, Nancy. Believe me, there's plenty to go around." Rick could hear the smile on Lynette's face though it was too dark to see. He reluctantly pulled himself free of Lynette's grip and felt Nancy urge him over onto his back on the bed, climbing on top of him, her hands pressed hard against his chest, lowering herself down onto his unyielding, wet member with excitement.

And it was then that Rick noticed that Nancy had adorned a satin Santa hat atop her wavy locks as she mounted him.

"I hear you're the new Mall Santa, Rickie boy."

He nodded and felt himself being plunged deeper and deeper into her with every stroke. She had already been well primed prior to him arriving. His body shook with pleasure as she continued.

"Well, Santa, you're in for a long night of receiving. I hope you've got a full sack because Nancy's been especially good this year."

Slick Rick was a firm advocate of naughty talk but the way she said the last line sent him into near ecstasy, grabbing at her round ass as she squealed out in pleasure and surprise, Rick grabbing up a handful of hair to pull her closer, his mouth on hers in moments.

He devoured her lips, tasting Lynette's sex on her mouth as well, his cock only getting harder with the new knowledge of her taste and smell. He rolled her over in one quick move, sliding out of her to turn her ass to him, sliding into her from behind. She let out a fantastic moan that would echo in his mind for weeks to come, smacking her ass to increase both their pleasure further.

"Santa doesn't care if you've been good, Nancy. He wants to see how bad you can be."

And that night, and many others to come until Christmas and beyond, Rick found out how bad both of they all could be.

And good nights were had by all. Or as good as they could be for Slick Rick and his crew of cougars.

The End

Explanation (*and apology*) to the Men:

All right, fuckers! It's time to give back to the women. No matter what you say, we, as men, must recognize that women play a significant role in these fantasies that have been created for you. We see it every day with the tabloids, the celebrities, as well as with all the other propaganda bullshit that is thrown out there for us men to latch on to and be even more of a consumer than we already are.

So, shouldn't we give them at least some gratitude for the greatness that they reward us with? Sure, they can be total bitches at times, but we go crazy for them, don't we?

So, without further ado, I present the last two stories: <u>Thugs and Kisses</u> and <u>How Santa Ate My Cookies</u> and I dedicate them to all the women that I have slept with and those that I haven't had the opportunity with yet.

May the merry blessings of the following stories send you into a thrilling climax, whether you are alone for the holidays and are curling up with this book or are having your man-bitch hold the book while you read it and play with yourself, thinking even nastier thoughts than I can write.

 Thugs and Kisses

Written by Titus Strong

CHAPTER ONE
~ "DO YOU HEAR WHAT I HEAR?" ~

"You like that, don't you, bitch?"

La 'Marcus Shaw had a big dick. There was no getting around that fact. You didn't have to tip toe around the subject with him or talk about his comfort zone with it. If anything, it was what controlled this man and not the brain in his head, if he even had one.

La 'Marcus drilled away at the young thing underneath him, hiking one of her legs up over his right shoulder so he could get a better angle with his massive member, hearing her call out to him, though he wasn't listening, not in the least. He had his feeling and he was getting it. Already, he had made her come two times but it didn't matter to him. He was waiting for his load to arrive. And, at the moment, he was getting closer than ever to it. Maybe that's why he didn't see his girlfriend come into the bedroom, frying pan in hand, aimed and at the ready just for him.

"Motherfucker! You a motherfucker!" Vanessa Long swung and made contact with La 'Marcus's shoulder just as he pulled his dick out of her younger sister, rolling off the bed, his naked ass knocking over the lamp next to the bedside table. It took him a minute to get his bearings, but he was up in no time.

"Bitch, what the fuck you think you're doing?"

Vanessa was fed up. Already, her baby daddy was a loser, dealing on the side out in the streets of Baltimore and had even brought home an S.T.D. months prior that she had to go to the doctor to get rid of, but this was the last straw. Her little sister, barely eighteen, sat up now, panting and covered in her older sister's bed sheets, hair messed up, a look of shame in her eyes.

Vanessa answered him back.

"**Bitch**? Who you calling **bitch**? I support your ass; I have for the last year. Watching your trifling ass sit up on my couch and eat up all my food! I take care of you and our three kids

and my little sister. But I see you want to take care of her now, too, huh?"

She kept the frying pan between her and La 'Marcus, making sure he was at least a few arm's length away. She had seen it before; been privy to the ravings of the angry, black man inside him.

"I put my money in!" He grabbed his boxers from the floor and slipped them on. Still, his large member was bulging out from underneath, throbbing from his lusty desires.

"Money?   You mean you put your DRUG money in! Motherfucker, I don't want you hustlin in my home, I already told you that! Now take your broke ass and get out!"

Vanessa knew where the line was with La 'Marcus; she had known since she had first met him when she was only nineteen. He had hit her then and put her in place some time ago, so she knew what to say and when not to say anything at all. She wished she had looked in his eyes a little bit better before coming at him just now because what she saw when she connected with them at that moment scared her more than anything had. She had messed with him while he was tripping.

He wasn't only a dealer but a user himself and, when he got fucked up, he was a son of a bitch. And, looking at him rushing at her, she knew this son of a bitch would need more than just a frying pan to be stopped. Nothing in the world could stop him now; not a speeding train, not that white cracker Superman, not even the police could stop the beating she was about to get. Vanessa dropped the frying pan and braced for impact.

*   *   *

Three days later, Vanessa woke to her three children standing next to her hospital bed, her younger sister with them. Her sister was clothed this time; different than the last time Vanessa had seen her, lying naked on her own bed with her man. The bad taste of that was still fresh in Vanessa's mouth.

Behind her children and her sister was an older white lady wearing a one-piece dress; very business-like.

Has to work for the government with an outfit like that, Vanessa thought, patting her youngest's head lightly, Jazmine nuzzling up to her mother's hand.

"Ms. Long, may I speak with you for a moment?"

It was all said and done after that. La 'Marcus got a couple of months for aggravated assault after he put Vanessa into a coma for three days, nearly giving her brain damage from the beating he had given her. The lady said that, just from the drugs La 'Marcus had in his system and that was found on the property, he would get some time.

But the fun didn't stop there. With the police called by Vanessa's sister, the apartment complex filed a complaint against her and gave her thirty days to vacate the premises on the grounds of breaking the contract with drug use on the property.

So, all in all, the holidays were turning out to be a real bitch. Vanessa found out that she had three broken ribs, a bruised jaw and left eye, a sprained left wrist, and some other cuts and bruises that the doctor said were minor.

But the real problem wasn't that, believe it or not. It was the friends of La 'Marcus that Vanessa was worried about.

Getting involved with a drug pusher was bad enough, but there was baggage with that as well.

Even if La 'Marcus was in jail for a few months, that wouldn't buy Vanessa and her family sufficient time to get away unless she moved to another state, which wasn't an option at the moment. But she had to get away from her old place as quick as possible. And that's where the white lady in the one-piece dress came in, her thin lips resolute and firm on her face.

"At the House of Ruth, we can protect you and your children from this, Ms. Long. If you give us a few weeks, we can do our best to have you placed in a home and with new employment so Mr. Shaw will be a distant memory in your lives. Would you like me to make the necessary calls, Ms. Long?"

This was so sudden. It seemed like only minutes ago that she was walking in to her apartment with bags full of food, getting tired of waiting for La 'Marcus and Chandra to come out and help unload the car.

They was too busy fucking; that's why their sorry asses weren't coming out to help!

Vanessa pictured again her little sister taking the full length of her man's dick in her and it nearly made her sick, thinking about how much older La Marcus was compared to her little sis. Vanessa was well aware that her sister was having sex with some of the thugs from the streets, bringing in a few choice thugs to fuck her right.

But my baby daddy, girl! That's fucked up!

Even her little sister could see the look in her eyes from a distance away. Chandra kept her nieces and nephew at bay while the House of Ruth representative spoke with Vanessa.

"I know these are some difficult things for you to think about. I'm going to leave you my card and give you a day or two to think about-"

"I don't need any more time. I've been wasting enough time as is. I'll take your help. I need to keep my kids safe."

"And yourself." The white lady began to write down some things on a clipboard she had sat down on the small end table next to Vanessa's bed.

"What?" Vanessa was still a bit groggy but she had forgotten about herself and her need for protection.

The representative continued. "Don't forget about yourself. The children need their mother, too. More than anything now, I believe. This is a moment of change, for the better. Your needs are important, too. Ms. Long!"

My needs are important. It had been years since she had thought of herself; her children, her boyfriend, her younger sister not having a place to stay after their parents died. It seemed so long ago that all of this had happened.

Vanessa felt the ache in her body, all of her limbs at once, kick in as the pain medication began to wear off. She looked at the lady again and then looked up to the ceiling of the room, taking a moment to try and remember when she had last thought of herself.

"My needs."

CHAPTER TWO
- "DO YOU SEE WHAT I SEE?" -

The white lady did as she had promised. Vanessa and her three children were moved counties away, to a smaller town away from the hustle and bustle of the one she had met La 'Marcus in, when all of her troubles had started. Vanessa's little sister Chandra stayed right where she was but moved in with some of her friends from school so Vanessa and her children could get back on their feet and adjusted.

Vanessa never heard from or about La 'Marcus except for when she had to go to court occasionally, but she didn't even look in his direction while in the courtroom. Being away from that world made it easier to get over all that craziness. In a few weeks, she was almost as good as new, the bruises having healed and gone down, the sprain and her ribs only a minor blip on the pain indicator.

And the location where she and her children were placed was nicer than she expected. She was given a room of her own and her three kids were given one next to hers with a bunk bed and twin bed on the other side of the room, complete with two writing desks on either side so the two oldest could do their homework when they came home from school.

Vanessa had even made a good friend. Ms. Dindem was an older, dark-skinned woman that cared for the oversized house and for its occupants. How Ms. Dindem was able to do that, Vanessa never quite knew. But she took care of business. The older lady said that it was because she had raised her own house full of children and even some grandchildren and it just came naturally. But she was a beast at cooking and cleaning.

Most women and their children stayed around ninety days and then moved on to their own new and improved lives. At least, that's what Vanessa had seen since being there the last month. Many times, she just sat at the breakfast table after the kids left, listening to other conversations had by the women that resided there, having cup after cup of coffee.

Other times, she would take her coffee out on the back porch and sit in one of the many rocking chairs, covered up in a blanket she had gotten from her room, looking out into the woods just behind the great big, three-story home located just off the main road.

But there were times, moments, when she was forced to get out for her own good by Ms. Dindem.

"Ms. Long, you've got to get out and start socializing again. You got to walk around with the rest of life that's moving along. Your wounds have healed; you look fine and you and your children are in a safe place now. There's no reason not to be moving forward in some way."

Vanessa retorted. "What if I just want to stay away from the world for a while? I mean, I've seen too much as a mother of three with a drug dealer as a baby daddy!"

Ms. Dindem took a moment to process all that the young woman said before answering.

"You have a good point, dear. But we all see and hear and things that we shouldn't have to. It doesn't mean that we have to stay in our shell forever. I'm not one to pry, but I've just noticed you just sort of sitting there, waiting for something to happen to you. Vanessa, dear, nothing's going to happen to you if you don't go out and get it for yourself. I ain't ever heard of anyone getting what they want just by sitting around!"

Ms. Dindem said this every day after breakfast once the kids were on the school bus and the dishes were being cleared away. And Vanessa answered back with the same thing, defending the shell she had put around herself.

This had gone on for the duration of her stay since she had been there, Vanessa growing tired of hearing it but keeping the respect of Ms. Dindem's opinion on the proverbial table, which was peppered with experience and knowledge far beyond what Vanessa could ever have. Then, one day, as all the women left from the kitchen one blustery day in December and left only Vanessa and the old woman there in the kitchen, she said something very out of character.

"Do you need a man, Vanessa?"

Vanessa didn't know what to say but retorted with, "What are you talking about, Ms. Dindem?"

"Do you need, you know, a physical release?" Vanessa had never heard anyone call an orgasm that before, so it took a minute for her mind to wrap around what Ms. Dindem was asking.

"What, you mean sex? Oh no, Ms. Dindem! I think I've had my fill of sex with any man for quite a while. In fact, I think I'm celibate now."

"Oh, hush, child! That's all nonsense! Everyone has needs and desires. It's our own responsibility to take care of those things, don't you think? Our needs?"

Needs. Meeting my needs. Here comes that word again.

"Are there even any men around here?" Vanessa hadn't seen a man since she had come to this house, with the exception of the random man at the supermarket when she went with Ms. Dindem to help her pick out and carry groceries.

"Oh, there's plenty of nooks and crannies that you find men around this town. There's a bar just a few miles down the street that's just teeming with lusty men. But we have a strict no-men policy here at the house. It's not just for the safety of the women, but some women have men issues that can encompass any and every man they see. We only have two or three men that come by and those are either shelter representatives or repair men. But they don't stay long enough to cause a problem. Plus, we've had them around for some time, so the women know all of them if they stay here long enough."

But still, Vanessa was resilient. She hadn't felt her woman parts move a pelvic muscle in some time. But, then again, she hadn't had the time to think about herself. Ms. Dindem continued.

"Well, if you need anything, feel free to go to the cleaning closet on the second floor. We put the key on a hook by the fridge. None of the kids can reach it and they don't even know what it unlocks. Just be sure to lock it behind you when you're done."

Vanessa raised an eyebrow, finishing up her coffee before putting the cup in the sink, rinsing it out.

"What does the key unlock?"

That would be a question that the answer to was far more interesting than anything Vanessa could have concocted in her head within her lifetime. Later that afternoon, just before her kids got home from school, she took the time to grab the old skeleton key from the hook by the fridge and walk up the flight of steps leading to the cleaning closet.

The door itself wasn't that far at all from her own. She was surprised that she had never taken notice of it before. But she had never seen anyone come out of it before. It was a much smaller door than the others, making it look like a broom closet or even a linen closet door.

That's why I never noticed it before. All in all, there was nothing to notice. It was just a plain, normal wooden door painted brown to match the other doors in the hallway. That's why what it held was all the more surprising.

The moment that Vanessa put the key in the door and opened it, she felt like a child, like she was doing something wrong, going somewhere where she wasn't allowed. And it felt nice. It wasn't the first time she felt this. Many times, in her youth, there were moments that she felt it important to put her defiance in the picture, to challenge the established order in control of her destiny.

But I was invited here. Why do I feel like I'm being naughty?

The room was completely dark when she entered but she could see a small string hanging from the ceiling directly in front of her from the little light that the hallway gave off. She walked in a little further and reached for the string, yanking it hard enough to for the light to switch on. And, when it did, Vanessa's eyes grew wide with surprise.

The entire room was, from shelves on the left to shelving on the right, full of sex toys. From dildos to vibrators of all kinds, bottles of lube, a rubber molded fist, butt plugs, porn DVDs in stacks of quantities 10 deep, special blankets still packaged that absorbed lubricants and other fluids that might stain a woman's bed.

Everything that Vanessa could imagine for a solo woman not wanting a man was there, including a few larger boxes with pictures on them of an entire chest and abs of a man body with "flesh-like" quality it said on the box, sporting an already hard dick that sprung up like an antenna for any passing woman to sit on if she so desired. All she had to do was take it out of the box and lube it up.

Immediately, Vanessa turned and shut the door behind her, locking it with one quick flick of her wrist.

I have an hour until my kids get home, she thought to herself, looking from shelf to shelf, making sure that her eyes didn't miss any details along the way.

The shelves on either side of her were six shelves high, with little dividers on each shelf that divided each toy/lubricant/butt plug from the other, showcasing each item in all its glory. It was as if an adult shop had dropped off all of its best items at the shelter for women, knowing it was going to be a tough road ahead for lonely vaginas.

So, this is what Ms. Dindem was talking about, taking care of our own needs! Damn, this is one way to do it!

The newly made single woman looked then at the porn collection still in plastic wrap from the manufacturer, even taking a few of them off the shelf to look at the back cover for further information. The titles alone were titillating.

"Big-booty hoes 7: A Hoe at Large, Ten inches and Coming: A Long, Hard look at Pleasure Palace, and **Between Rock Hard and a Soft Place."**

There were easily over 50 different titles to choose from, many of them more about empowerment in the bedroom than many she had seen in her life. Vanessa had never been really much of a porn watcher. She did, however, have a toy. It was something small, something that could be hidden well from the kids and any other prying eyes. La 'Marcus never knew about it. It was a battery-operated rabbit; a powder blue one.

She had gotten it years ago when they first came out and it hit so many spots that she became loud at the amount of pleasure it could give her, so much that she had to take it out with her, away from the house so she could make her noise elsewhere.

The elsewhere ended up being in her parked car down the street in an abandoned bank parking lot. She always parked and pushed the rabbit down into her panties, one hand on the wheel while the other was guiding the rabbit down the rabbit hole.

She wasn't against taking one of the toys now, just to try it out.

What's the worst thing that could happen, right?

Chapter Three
- "Do you know what I know?" -

It had been a long time since Vanessa had been naughty. But looking at all of those toys and even taking one for herself, it did a bit to boost her libido in a way she had not felt in some time. In the quiet of her room before the rest of the women and children had gotten home, Vanessa used the toy. It was much better than her little rabbit she had left back at her old place.

Goodbye to old bedfellows, Vanessa thought to herself as she felt the first of two orgasms hit her from the vibrator she had taken from the broom closet. It was a little bit bigger than the rabbit she had and it was a fiery orange and yellow. The outside package labeled it `The Phoenix`, with a little

And rise it did. No sooner had she felt that last of the desire from her first orgasm subsiding, tears still in the corner of her eyes from the pleasure that pulsed within her, than the second could be felt stirring within, from underneath a great sheltered place that only the edge of her Phoenix could reach.

The Phoenix was different than the rabbit she had used because it had a little rubber tip no bigger than her thumb that fit snugly inside her, keeping the vibration not just on the surface of her clitoris, but reverberating just inside of her as well, forcing her to grab her pillow and stuff it in her mouth as the shockwaves of pleasure rolled over her body with each passing vibration.

Oh fuck! Damn, what did I get myself in to? Vanessa turned off the vibrating Phoenix and let the pleasure subside between her legs. She pulled the pillow under her head as she rested in the moment of bliss before the reality around her took over.

But the wells of pleasure within her would not be still. Inside, maybe somewhere she tried her best to hide away, she awakened more than just the need for The Phoenix. A place that she had not thought about in a long time now came to the surface of her mind.

She remembered some time ago taking the pleasure that she wanted and making it her own, before all of the craziness of the life around her got in the way. She remembered just being a woman with a man, and those two people devoured one another for countless nights.

Vanessa wasn't just thinking about La' Marcus and their time together but of the other men she had bedded in the past and what they had brought to the table.

An insurmountable load of pleasure between us.

That's what she remembered right now. She missed the light touches that started it all as well as the rough, animalistic clawing at one another that ended it, loving even more what was encompassed in the in between. She hadn't been treated like a desirous, lust-filled woman in a long time.

And times were about to change. Right now.

After putting her toy away in a safe place, a clothes drawer with all of her clothes folded in it, she gathered herself up and straightened her hair, getting up from the bed.

Ms. Dindem was easily found before the children arrived from the school bus. The old woman smiled when she saw the look on Vanessa's face.

"Well, dear. You're looking quite better. You look like you want to say something."

And, indeed, the young mother of three did want to say something. So much more than she ended up saying, really.

"Is it okay if I go out for a couple of hours? Would you mind watching my babies?"

Ms. Dindem shook her head adamantly.

"It will be no trouble at all, Ms. Long. I'd be happy to watch them myself. In fact, they can help me with unloading the groceries and making dinner for tonight. Will you be back in time for dinner?"

Vanessa pulled out her winter coat from the coat closet by the door.

"I don't think so. But I should be back tonight. I just want to get out for a while. I thought about what you said, about getting out and socializing with the rest of the world. You're right."

Ms. Dindem was as pleased with herself as a woman her age could ever be. A look of surprise passed across her face and then it was gone, replaced by the humbled look that Vanessa was used to seeing.

"Oh, well, that's good, hon. I'm glad you've had a change of heart. Getting out for a little while will help you feel better. Be sure to eat something while you're out."

Vanessa nodded and went out the door, closing it behind her.

I'll be sure to, Ms. Dindem. Starting with dessert first!

Vanessa climbed into her car and started driving.

She said it was only a few miles from here, Vanessa reminded herself, keeping on the main road that led into town. And the old ladies' directions had been correct. The little dive bar that she had spoken of earlier was just on the corner, tucked away from the street just enough that it hid itself away quite well, Vanessa having to pull a U-turn at the next traffic light to get back to it.

Happy Times was a hole in the wall type of bar with a series of televisions posted up in its corners in a desperate attempt to be something that it wasn't; a sports bar. It had a few jerseys and football helmets framed in shadow boxes on the walls of local teams in the area, but nothing from bigger teams, making the place as noncommittal as possible.

The rest of the bar, as Vanessa entered, looked to be of the same stock as any other small-town bar could be: there was a wrap-around bar that was rectangular shaped in the middle room and a few circular tables that were scattered throughout the surrounding areas left over, a few people in clusters here and there. There was even a small section that had booths to the left, the lighting a little bit dimmer, a bit more discreet than at the bar.

Vanessa moved over to the bar, taking a seat on a stool not far from the bartender, a hefty, burly man polishing mugs with a dry, white cloth.

"What can I get for the lady tonight?"

"Do you have pink moscato?" The bartender nodded.

"That we do. Glass or bottle?"

"A glass, please. A big girl glass of it."

He smiled at her, grabbing a long wine glass from above the bar. He sat it down in front of her and grabbed a chilled bottle from underneath the bar.

"A big girl glass of pink moscato, coming up. Would the lady like to see a menu?"

Vanessa shook her head. "No, not at the moment. I'll be fine with the drink for now."

"Well, let me know if you need anything else." The portly bartender topped off her glass and moved away to another party at the other end of the bar, a couple giggling and laughing about something Vanessa couldn't quite hear.

She sipped on her wine, taking her first drink of alcohol in some time, enjoying the moment away from reality, from where she had been the last few weeks, what she had barely escaped from with La' Marcus and the rest of the mess that followed along with him. She didn't notice that her glass was empty until the bartender was in front of her again, holding up the bottle of pink moscato.

"Can I get the lady another glass? And it's Nick."

"Thank you, Nick. Sure, I'll have another. I didn't even notice that I had finished."

He topped off her glass again, putting the bottle back under the counter in the cooler.

"They never do those that are lost in thought. And the lady is lost deeply in it today."

"Is that a bad thing though?" She sipped at the second glass a little slower than the first, though the taste of it was delicious.

"No, not at all. Actually, I think people should be lost in thought more often; gives them perspective on everything that's going on around them. And it gives me a job." Nick smiled at her and left her alone with her thoughts then, moving to a new crowd that had come in through the front door.

"Just have a seat where you like, ladies and gentlemen. A server will be with you shortly."

After three big girl glasses of pink moscato, the sun was already setting in the pinkish-blue sky. It was mid-December and everything around her went dark at around 5:30 p.m., Vanessa's night turning out nothing like she had planned.

I could have done better picking up men at the grocery store with Ms. Dindem.

There were no men to be had all except for the middle-aged Nick, who was looking more and more attractive by the moment.

Maybe he could give me a run for my money, Vanessa thought, but then thought better of it. *He probably doesn't like chocolate at all. Probably never thought about it.* She chuckled at this idea, of her and some older man a completely different race and background from her going at it. Even half-drunk, she had trouble picturing it without laughing.

That's why she didn't notice the man that sat down at the bar next to her until his voice broke through the background banter that surrounded her.

"Rum and coke, Nick. And keep'em coming."

Vanessa could hear Nick's response somewhere in the bar and, in a few moments, saw the middle-aged bartender passing a young set of hands a full glass of alcohol. When she turned to get a quick view of the man next to her, she was nearly shocked off of her bar stool.

He was a light-skinned dream. His smile caught her attention first. From the corner of his mouth, the smile came. There was a hint of it at first, his lips barely parting to get the first sip of rum down, his deep blue eyes darting over to Vanessa for a moment and then back to the television screen mounted on a wall in front of him. He put down his drink and she could see the full smile and all its splendor.

The rest of him was just as fine as the smile, but it was hard to take notice of because Vanessa's mind was swimming within the sea of moscato she had already jumped into. He had hair cut close to his head and a small line of facial hair around his mouth and up to his ears. When he spoke to her, it took all she had inside to respond.

"Hi. I'm Tony. What's your name?" He reached his hand out to her.

When she took it into her own, there was a charge of energy that pulsed through her so strong that it was hard for her to contain.

"I'm Vanessa."

"Nice to meet you, Vanessa."

Vanessa had no idea that she would be fucking him less than an hour later.

The unisex bathroom was never a good idea in a bar, but it worked to their advantage for what they were doing. Vanessa grabbed at the buttons on his shirt and began undoing one at a time, doing her best to keep herself from ripping his shirt off.

"Are you sure about this, Vanessa?" She could feel Tony's breath on her neck, urging her back down from her lustful appetite. She wanted him and there was nothing that he could say that would change that. After the first kiss at the bar, her body was aching for something strong to take it over. And Tony fit the bill just right.

"No, I want this! I want you!" She felt his lips press against her own as he shut and locked the door behind them, Tony sitting her up on the sink countertop, lifting up the dress she wore to get to her panties. His strong hands were on the lace panties in no time, drawing them down her legs and off and away from the low heels that she wore, tossing them on the counter behind her, his hands pulling her closer.

"I want you, too, Vanessa." And that's when she felt the excitement he had contained rather well in his jeans. Her hands guided themselves down to the belt at his waist, pulling on the clasp to open them the rest of the way, unzipping and pulling his jeans and briefs down in one, quick movement. And there it was; his hard, thick cock, the head of his cock pulsing in anticipation for what was about to happen. Her hands found it without looking, keeping her focus on his lips with her own, his eyes burning a hole through the shell she had built up over time, her desire taking over with a little help from her liquid courage from earlier.

And from The Phoenix. From the ashes...

As he slid on protection and pressed himself into her, Vanessa realized that even her toy couldn't prepare her for the pleasure she would allow herself in the bathroom of a seedy bar.

"Take it, Tony! Take it!" Tony held onto the countertop and grabbed a handful of her hair in his other hand, slamming into her desirous frame, over and over, Vanessa squeezing her legs around his hips, her hands working their way up and around his shoulders as her body shook with pleasure. She felt his mouth on her neck, his teeth grazing her skin, his breath coming in labored gasps of desire, one of his hands uncovering her breasts from underneath the dress, her naked form pressing against his own as he quickened his pace.

She knew nothing about this man. He knew nothing about her. They had nothing that she knew of in common. The only thing she knew at this very moment was that she needed this, needed him, never wanted him to stop his want for her.

But her body exploded then, sending her legs into a fit of motions that tightened around his waist, expelling the breath from his body, her fingers digging into his back, her face pressing into the crook of his neck.

"I'm coming for you, Tony. You're making me come." His body settled into deep thrusts then, prolonging her orgasm, drawing it out of her as she had never felt it drawn out before. She let her entire body feel it. It was much stronger than what her toy had done earlier. The Phoenix had only opened the doors to the pleasure.

She stepped all the way through the doors now.

In a few moments, as her orgasm began to subside, one of Tony's deep thrusts remained inside and his gripped tightened on her, his breath coming out in an almost inaudible whisper.

"I'm coming for you, too. Oh fuck, girl!" She could feel his throaty whisper against her chest, sending her body into a quivering state of chill bumps and tingles of pleasure. She could taste the rum from his lips on her own as she leaned back against the countertop, taking a breath for the first time in a long number of seconds, breathing in their mingling scents.

It was then that they finally heard the knock on the door; the knock that had started some time ago and lingered there as they pleasured one another. Tony reluctantly let her go and they did their best to appear unfettered and not covered in each's sex and sweat from the last previous minutes.

But their eyes made contact then and Tony drew himself close to her as Vanessa was still attempting to get dressed, pressing his mouth against hers. She wrapped her arms around his neck and pulled him closer as well, putting her own passion into the kiss until the knocks came somewhat harder than before, both of them scrambling to get their clothes on.

When they finally opened the door, Nick was standing a few feet away, trying to keep the prying eyes of his other patrons from seeing them.

"I just need to make sure you guys pay your tab."

Tony and Vanessa both blushed as they closed the door behind them and walked back to their stools at the bar.

Chapter Four
· Sleepless Nights ·

Ms. Dindem was right; there were no men around the house. After that night Vanessa spent at Happy Times, there was a drought of seeing any men for a while. She didn't even see a single man at the grocery store the last two times she had gone with Ms. Dindem, with the exception of a few teenage boys bagging groceries and getting carts from the parking lot.

She had heard from the other women at the shelter home that a Mr. Fix-It would be coming for his monthly visit. Several of the women went about to fixing their hair and getting their nicest outfits with the best bra that showed their goodies without really showing their goodies all the way. And that's when Vanessa understood; he had to be an attractive, single guy. She had seen this all too many times; the limited number of women all ogling over one man.

This will not end well, Vanessa thought to herself, helping Ms. Dindem fold the rest of the linen that day, trying to find something constructive to do that wouldn't send her into a stir-crazy rage. Lately, Vanessa being cooped up in the same place had began to get to her.

So, when the first mention of a man coming to the shelter surfaced, Vanessa felt a twinge of excitement, like she was a child going to the zoo to see an endangered animal all locked in its cage. She made sure that her hair was near perfect, that her lipstick was on point and shadowed the contours of her lips. She found a comfy bra and a sundress that showed off her well-lotioned, shaved legs.

What am I doing, being as childish as the other women, Vanessa reasoned, ushering her children downstairs to watch television in the living room so they would be close by when Mr. Fix-it came in.

So, it was best to say that she was a little bit surprised to see that Mr. Fix-it was none other than Tony, the guy she had fucked only a few weeks back. His face housed the shock of seeing her a little better than her own. She had to close her gaping mouth when she first saw him enter with the toolbox and tool belt, moving into the kitchen area where the problem areas were said to be. One of the women at the shelter passed by her, smiling.

"Isn't he good-looking? And I hear he's single." The woman was just a giddy as a school girl, using one of her hands to check her hair while the other hefted up her ample bosom a little further so that her cleavage could be seen more clearly.

And he was good-looking. Vanessa knew that the night they had picked each other up and lost all control. He was light-skinned and had his hair shorn closely to his scalp, leaving only a little bit of hair on top. He had only a small line of facial hair and reached from just in front of his ears down to his chin, almost as thin as the hair atop his head. He had a muscular build that couldn't be hidden easily by clothes. He could be a cover model of a fashion magazine if it weren't for his country living flannel shirt and fitted corduroys that he wore as he sauntered in.

He took a quick passing glance at Vanessa and flashed a smile to her, nodding his head.

"Ma'am." He made his way into the kitchen and was tearing apart the kitchen sink in no time, making his runs back and forth to his repair truck as needed throughout the afternoon for parts.

Vanessa didn't get any time in with him that day. There was a swarm of single women that kept 'needing something' from the kitchen, finding any and every excuse to get within eyeshot of this piece of living, breathing man meat before them.

It was as if they had never seen a man before, Vanessa remarked, moving back to the living room with her kids to watch t.v. She could hear the girlish giggles that the women made when they struck up conversation with Mr. Fix-it in the kitchen, Ms. Dindem trying her best to keep the crowd away as he worked, looking a bit embarrassed at the situation when she came into the living room to sit for a minute.

"Have you ever seen anything like it? It's as if they don't remember at all why they are here in the first place and lost all sense about them." She wiped the sweat off her brow with a clean dishrag she had in her hand and looked over at Vanessa.

"You're the only one that seems to have it together, Vanessa. They should take a lesson from you, my dear. I knew that night out would do you good."

And, in another moment, Ms. Dindem was back in the kitchen, waving the salivating women away with her dishrag, soon ushering Mr. Tony up to another place that needed fixing.

If you only knew what it did for me, Ms. Dindem, then you wouldn't be so quick to judge my response to that hunk of a man that you've got there with you, Vanessa thought, trying her best to keep her composure.

But, somewhere, in the most private of places, her body was aching for Tony to have his way with her, to take her and put his hands on her, to touch her in ways that made her feel wanted and desired, as he had that night at the bar.

He walked past without a look or a word and followed Ms. Dindem up the steps, moving to the bathrooms to check on things up there next. Vanessa could hear a shuffle of feet from the women getting in their places upstairs.

I'm sure they're looking for their moment to accidentally go into the bathroom to get another peek at the man in their presence; in their domain. Within arm's reach.

Vanessa shifted in her place on the couch, doing her best not to let his presence get to her. But, no matter what she did, the moments of the past brought her right back to his smell. His touch.

His thrusts. The final moans of pleasure as he spilled himself inside of her. He was well-protected that night but she could still feel the swelling of him before he erupted and the convulsions that his thick member made inside of her, bringing her own body to climax upon his in a glorious, lust-filled finale.

But Vanessa hadn't see any of that in his eyes now. There was nothing to show that they had known each other in any capacity at all. It was as if it were a dream of some sorts, a sick fantasy brought about by that fiery sex toy that day and that room full of naughtiness.

Mr. Fix-it came and went after fixing what needed to be fixed, not saying a single word to her while he was there. The women in the house sat in mild disappointment that night that he hadn't stayed longer, that the kitchen sink didn't spray water on him so he'd have to take off his shirt, or that he hadn't shown any of them attention while he was there. This and other conversations were had about the man that had come, but all was settled by the time dinner was eaten and everyone was going to their rooms to get ready for bed that evening.

It had been some time since Vanessa had been alone to herself. In the past, La 'Marcus was always there with his friends or her little sis was always bringing her loud ass friends up in her place. But here, in the safe house, it was quiet. All in all, it was a nice place to stay.

To get away from things, Vanessa thought to herself, checking in on her three children before she went to bed herself.

They were all asleep, wrapped up tight and safe from harm. It was only ten o'clock but they were already asleep as well. Vanessa pulled her bathrobe up over her shoulders tighter and pulled the robe cord a little so she didn't feel a draft through it.

It was getting colder, Vanessa agreed, looking outside the window not far from her own bed. She had made herself snugger in her own bed as well, having doubled up on her comforter in the last few days to keep the warmth in once she got under it. It was only a few days from Christmas now and they were due to leave for protective custody once the trial was over, which was planned to be shortly after the New Year. There was frost on the windowpanes and just outside on the other building across from them. No snow had come down yet.

It usually didn't until after Christmas. Even to think that any snow would come down after Thanksgiving was ludicrous. But times are changing. Stranger things have been known to happen. It was during times like these that Vanessa really appreciated having a man around; a warm, comfortable body next to hers, easily guiding it from a moment of sleep to an act of passion in one precise movement.

Then she remembered Tony's guiding hand on her back as they found their way into the bar bathroom. He was himself a strong and firm man, like an oak, presenting a never-faltering picture to all the women at the shelter.

But that touch...

Parts of that touch alone had thrilled Vanessa to no end. Tony wasn't simply a man on a mission but he had sensitivity and charm. Just from those few, however brief, moments, Vanessa knew he had a soul and an essence more than most.

Thinking of these things easily brought on her desire, in a place that she had just started to get to know again after being away from it for so long. She returned to her bed, returned to the warmth that was soon there with her, as well as the continued thoughts of Tony, a.k.a. Mr. Fix-it, and his bright eyes, those that looked on her with -

How exactly did his eyes look on me? With desire? Lust? Want? No, that couldn't be it. Mr. Tony wanted no part of a broken woman. It was just a fling, a single moment of weakness that the alcohol had helped along. And, as for here, he was simply doing his part to help, what he felt was help to those that needed it.

But, deep down inside, Vanessa didn't mind in the least thinking on that night pressed up against the bathroom sink, taking each deserving thrust by that man.

Dammit, I wish I could use my toy now! No matter how much Vanessa wished it, she wasn't able to take out her vibrating apprentice at her bedside because it would make far too much noise. She had put it away for the time being; The Phoenix was packed away with all the other items she had brought with her from her old place.

And it was desperately needed at this time, Vanessa reminded herself, feeling the throbbing ache begin between her legs as it kept her from drifting off to sleep, pulsing almost as a request for release.

The fingers of her right hand soon found the throbbing and did their best to abate it, moving slowly at first, almost serenely. There was one thought and it was of pleasure and being pleased. She had no one there to help with it and was extremely hesitant to think of anyone worthy of her moans.

But Tony was worthy. He had been worthy of them. Damn, he had worked hard for them.

Her pace quickened.

As her well of desire deepened, she applied pressure to any sensitive spot she could find and, turning her head into her pillow, breathed a deep, sexy breath of urgency as her orgasm erupted out onto her courageous middle finger, her eyelids fluttering as the waves of pleasure passed through her. She calmed her hand's movement down a bit and let the pleasure subside. And, as Vanessa pulled her hand away from her pleasure spot, her mind quickly gave her the image of Tony coming in from a wintry afternoon.

Off with the gloves, the snow boots, the hat and scarf. All other items dropped quickly as well, in a fast yet slow, dream-like motion and, soon, his warm and inviting hands were all over her naked, waiting form in front of him.

And Vanessa's right hand stayed where it was then, her middle finger and a few others continuing to play. His hands were on her, soft at first, just as her strokes began against her clit, then his hands put her into position to take his own throbbing dick, the strokes now forceful and constant.

Vanessa imagined his hands on her hips and she climaxed again in minutes, biting on the pillow next to her, her thighs clenching down on her hand, her mind awash in pleasure and the smells of what Tony and his sex would smell like. It had been some time since she had climaxed so quickly.

And, that night, Vanessa slept soundly, just the thoughts of

Mr. Fix-it and a few fingers bringing her to her high point.

Chapter Five
- The Thrilling Climax -

Days came and went and Christmas Eve had managed to sneak up on Vanessa without her really knowing it was here. In all of the coming weeks after having been put in the woman's shelter, she had practically forgotten it was the holiday season. The hum of her new toy and the buzz she had gotten from that night in the bar with Mr. Fix-it had all but subsided. She had even found her place while at the women's shelter.

She had always loved to cook. Her specialty was desserts. From pecan pies to sweet potato pie to cakes and shortbread cookies, she had become a master in her own time, learning from her grandmother while she had still been alive, watching on a stool in the kitchen since she was just a little girl. She practically lived in the kitchen with her granny, or as everyone would call her 'Gram-Gram'. But it wasn't until she came here, with a large group that considered her family, that Vanessa was able to use her talents in the kitchen again.

In a few days, Vanessa and her children would be leaving. The first and second court appearance came and went and, with it, it placed her far away from the reach of La' Marcus Shaw and any of his thug friends. Vanessa and her children would be safe and sound a few cities away. She had even been guaranteed job placement once she got there. Yes, things were looking up for her and her children.

While the children all went out Christmas shopping at the mall with the help of local community sponsors that Ms. Dindem had found, Vanessa stayed and was hard at work in the kitchen, something she had no problem doing now that she was alone with her thoughts and the many ingredients that lay scattered across the kitchen counters.

All of the Vanessa of old had come back full force and she had spent hours in the kitchen, mixing ingredients, baking dozens of her specialties at a time; cupcakes, cookies, whole pies, and cobblers of all flavors.

However, she had not stopped fantasizing about Tony at all during these stints of culinary work in the kitchen. At times, when he would come by and drop things off for the house or fix up the Christmas decorations in each room and outside, Vanessa would find herself trying to stay in the kitchen as much as possible. She didn't know if she was scared of him or what he would see in her face if he looked into it. But he came and went just as he had done that first time to fix the sink. If he had seen anything, he didn't say anything to her or anyone else.

He didn't care one bit about some worn out lady with three kids, Vanessa told herself, getting back to the baking, the ingredients, and all of the other things she had kept herself busy with the last few days.

There were 45 people staying at the shelter since Vanessa had been there. The amount of food that they consumed was overwhelming sometimes, not to mention the amount of celebrations that were had for those that were leaving or some that were coming in. With that many people in one place, there was always a birthday, anniversary that overtook them to tears that they tried best to forget; so Vanessa did what she did best. She baked.

Sometimes she would spend all afternoon in the kitchen with others helping her. They would mix the ingredients or place them out for her. Then she would be off and away, in her own Candy Land, moving through the recipes, making more than she ever had in her life. She was one determined woman.

That's why she didn't see Mr. Fix-it standing at the corner of the kitchen that night, staring straight at her. Well, staring at her ass.

"You are one determined woman in here! Cooking up a storm!"

The strength in his voice nearly scared her out of her apron. She caught a quick breath and covered her chest with her free hand, setting down the mixing spatula.

"You scared the daylights out of me!"

Tony's face seemed quickly apologetic. So did his voice, which was lowered somewhat the next time he spoke.

"I'm sorry, Vanessa. I was only watching you work." He walked a few steps into the kitchen.

"I've never seen a woman work such magic in the kitchen."

"Well, that's quite a compliment coming from you."

"Listen, I think we need to talk, Vanessa."

She looked over at him, trying her best not to draw herself into those eyes.

"About what, Mr. Tony?"

"About the night at the bar." She stopped mixing and crossed him to pour the ingredients into a baking pan near him. He moved out of the way, but only a little, still intent on getting her attention while he had it. This was the first time that they had been alone since that night.

"Vanessa, listen. I didn't know you were here. If I did, if we had talked more- "

"What? You'd have done what exactly? Steered clear of me because I was a damaged woman?"

He looked at Vanessa as though she were crazy. "What? No, of course not! I didn't know your situation. You looked as though you had everything together and was just looking for company."

Vanessa finished with the ingredients and put the baking pan into one of the free ovens, setting the timer on it.

"I **was** looking for company. And you were, too. That's why it worked out so well for the both of us. What else is there to talk about?"

Tony moved closer to her, close enough for Vanessa to smell the scent of him. Even in a kitchen full of baked goods and desserts, she could decipher his smell from all the others. And it drove her crazy. She kept all this on the inside, with the exception of her gaze, which now moved to his lips as he spoke.

"I can't stop thinking about you, Vanessa. Everything we did that night echoes in my mind. I thought I would never see you again. I nearly died when I saw you here. I didn't know what to say. But now I do." He pressed himself up against her and Vanessa had trouble resisting. She backed herself up against the kitchen counter.

"What are you doing, Tony?"

"I want you, Vanessa. I can't help myself when I'm around you."

He leaned in to kiss her and she scooted back against the counter as far as she could, one of her hands pressing against one of her baked goods. The chocolate cream topping smeared against her hand but she was too preoccupied to notice, keeping herself at bay with the man that had been in her thoughts ever since they left the bar that night.

The next few moments would forever live in Vanessa's mind.

Vanessa had never been able to get into a mood that would ever allow her to think of food as sexy. But, as Tony licked the toppings off the little bit of wrist the chocolate cream had touched, his tongue lapping up the rest of the cream as slowly as possible, his eyes still on hers, there was a spark that erupted between her legs. It was so strong that it made her adjust her legs a bit closer to one another, hoping to capture it and hold it as long as humanly possible.

Then Vanessa felt his teeth on the tip of her palm, igniting the spark again, this time sending a stronger jolt up through her thighs. He pressed his fingers down firmly on her legs and kept them open, a space for him to get even closer to her.

Already, Vanessa was in the midst of panting from the heat coming off of her, her newly cleaned hand slipping back to brace herself as Mr. Tony unbuttoned the side of the skirt, slipping it down off her legs and discarding it on the floor. She barely had any energy to fight but she still spoke.

"What do you think you're doing, Tony?"

In the dim light of the kitchen, among the festive cakes and pies, cookies, and other confectionary goods, Mr. Tony's smile nearly made all of it melt.

"You know that shudder you just felt? Yeah, well, I'm about the help it along. And I've been wanting to taste you for weeks now, so it seems that it's kind of killing two birds with one stone." He continued down her thighs, past her knees, his lips grazing the insides of her leg, her body a little hesitant when it came to being devoured in the kitchen when anyone could come in.

His voice did not break, his tone did not waver. In it were all the finest intricacies of a man that Vanessa had wanted, all rolled into one. And, as her pink panties flew off the tip of his fingers and into the air, she realized that he wanted her just as badly as she wanted him.

Nothing was fast. Tony didn't rush the moments he gave her. Though the kids and the rest of the parents could be back at any moment, it seemed in Tony's eyes that they had all night. And from the way that he drove his tongue into her, lapping up the wetness he had created, he was planning on keeping her busy from her present kitchen duties for an extended amount of time.

She did her best to lean back for him. However, with all of the desserts and other treats still on display and half-finished on the counter, she kept herself propped up on her elbows, her legs wrapped tightly around Tony's shoulders, his strong arms picking her ass up off the counter from time to time, when his tongue had stroked a spot that made her tighten on him. Those soon became the norm, Vanessa grabbing at the edges of the counter to hold herself steady.

"You gonna make me come soon, Tony. Is that what you want?" The strokes with his tongue became harder, more focused then, his urgency catching her off guard, her fingers slipping off the edge of the counter, Tony's shoulders holding her in place.

The spark was there, hovering over the tip of his tongue. Electric pulses charged up and down her body, into her fingertips, forcing her eyes to close, her head tilted back to receive the pleasure. Another stroke from the tip of his tongue was all it took. Vanessa's legs tightened, her body began to shake and the most desirous moan escaped her lips, making her lips numb in the process.

Tony tightened his grip on Vanessa's thighs and lapped his tongue across her already sensitive clit, sending her hands into a frenzy for a hold, trying to keep him steady but, at the same time, trying to keep the sensation at bay.

There was no helping it. Her orgasms overlapped, the second one coming in a wave so strong that she lost the balance she had maintained on her elbows, feeling her back press down hard against the gingerbread cookies, their fragile, little bodies snapping easily underneath her, half a tray of them pressing into her skin.

They were still warm, the cookies.

"Mis—mist—mister...Ton—" It hurt it felt so fucking good. Vanessa let go of the world around her. She let the cheating gangster-ass ex-boyfriend, the trifling little sister, her children and their rough predicament, her job (or lack thereof); all of it went out the fucking window. The only thing that she thought of, besides those poor cookies, was her pulsing clit and the tongue that wouldn't give it a minute of down time.

After her legs relaxed, she felt Tony moving away from her pulsing juice box and head back up towards the rest of her body, his lips still hovering over the exposed skin of her thighs. It was no longer sensitive or ticklish, but buzzing with a desire for him to devour ever part of her that he saw fit to.

There was a slight smile at the corners of his mouth.

Vanessa didn't have the energy to smile. The whole of her body was smiling at him, an outward glow, a smell of desire and of what was to come lingering in the air, even permeating through the festive smells in the kitchen that had begun since this morning when she turned the oven on.

But something was simmering inside my own oven, Vanessa thought to herself, doing her best to look somewhat presentable in such a state. But there was no way to look sexy amongst the broken pieces of gingerbread, the tumbled sprinkles, chocolate glaze half emptied out onto the kitchen counter she still mounted, held only by her legs and by Mr. Tony.

She felt one of his warm hands moving across her stomach then, running across the thin layer of sweat that sat upon the surface of her skin. His fingers found the clasp of her bra behind her back and unclasped it easily, both of his hands on her holiday-appropriate attire.

"I need this off for what I want to do, Vanessa."

"And what's that, Mr. Tony?"

"Humor me for a moment." Vanessa was in mid-nod when she felt the head of his cock slide into her, penetrating all the way back to her pelvic wall with the first thrust.

"Oh, fuck, Mr. Tony! You're so deep!"

But that was not the only thing Tony had in store. Vanessa looked into his eyes and saw much more. In one hand, he had a small metal container of chocolate sauce, pouring a little bit on her inner left thigh, propping her leg up over his shoulder.

The chocolate sauce slid lazily down her leg and rounded to the back of her thigh, Tony's mouth soon after the trailing beads of deliciousness, his cock sliding out an inch or so then slamming deep inside her again, catching Vanessa off guard, her eyes still trained on the last little drip of chocolate sauce that Tony's exquisite tongue lapped up, her lips quivering at the idea that his tongue could have her coming again in a moment's notice.

Tony continued, saucing her right thigh and doing the same, watching Vanessa this time with his own eyes, the head of his dick simultaneously dipping down deep and then slowly filling her up all the way again, over and over. The build-up was excruciatingly good. Tony took his time.

More men need to be like this, Vanessa noted, the gingerbread cookies under her nothing but holiday debris now, her back pressed hard against the kitchen counter as Mr. Tony slammed into her faster, his strokes bringing her pleasure centers back as the head of his member rubbed against them time and again.

And, time and again, Vanessa lost herself in the sensation, in the lightning that arced itself through her body as she climaxed, Tony keeping his steady pace until her legs ceased their jerking and her body softened around him again.

The calm after the storm, Vanessa thought to herself, spreading herself across the kitchen counter the rest of the way, cookie trays, half-baked goods, ingredients of all kinds scattering themselves to the corners, some even tipping off the edges and tumbling to the floor.

"How did you like that, Vanessa?"

Vanessa purred in response, her whole body relaxed, even with the veritable mess around them.

"That was rather yummy."

It wasn't until Ms. Dindem cleared her throat that the two of them took notice that they weren't alone anymore. The old lady's hands were full of groceries that Vanessa had asked for to finish the last of the desserts.

The old lady smiled at the two of them and spoke, a small mixture of giggles coming out as she did so.

"I don't know about you, Vanessa, but I was thoroughly entertained. And you have about five minutes to get appropriate before the kids and the rest of the women get home."

The End

How Santa Ate My Cookies

Written by Titus Strong

<u>Footnote</u>: (Yeah, cause I'm like that!)

Christmas is such a wonderful time, don't you think? But for those in the Armed Forces stationed overseas, patrolling territories that are on the regular a dangerous and sometimes life-sacrificing responsibility, not so much.

But hey, soldiers find a way to make due during the holidays. And this story is for them; to the soldiers that only get glory in the papers and news. I'm writing this story for you.

Now, you will not only be a hero in my eyes, but a bunch of pervs hell-bent on getting your nut off, which I already knew anyway because I was one just like you!

Enjoy and Hoooah!

CHAPTER ONE
- THE SET UP -

Corporal Justine Hicks knew where her faith lay in regards to Christmas. She had spent a great many Christmases with her family in Akron, Ohio and knew **that** was where she wanted to be right now. No one could count the amount of tears that she had shed since being here in Kabul, Afghanistan, and she knew she had a few more buckets to fill before she left early next year. It being late December, with Christmas Eve rapidly approaching, everyone on post was getting antsy. All the soldiers, both male and female, wanted nothing more than to be home with their families, but knew that their duties lay in other places at the moment.

But the places that the soldiers frequented, the mess hall, the administrative office, and the common area were at least giving off a slight sense of home when everyone entered them; they were adorned with festive items that the soldiers had received from care packages to prepare for a long Christmas holiday away from home.

There were stockings hung in the mess hall with care with a slew of different names on them written in black magic marker. There were also wreaths placed on all of the interior entrances of the corridors and some bright, metallic green Christmas paper wrapped around the doors and some of the dimly lit windows, giving the rooms a Christmassy feel.

And, last but not least, there was a tree. It wasn't a Charlie Brown tree, either, all emaciated and nearly needleless. Someone had taken great pains to send bits and pieces of the 7-foot artificial tree through the mail, shipping off individual pieces over a period of weeks, getting the last few pieces there before Thanksgiving so all of the soldiers could help decorate the tree with the selection of ornaments that came in their other care packages.

Justine looked at the tree now, in the administration office, in the early morning hours just after P.T., the office still in its throngs to start the morning up. It had a great many ornaments on it, making each artificial limb sag a bit more than it should. There were ornaments from all over the United

States, some in the shape of each state while others were pictures of family in little ornament frames. And, not far up the tree, was a little frame with her family smiling out at her, surrounded by a green acrylic Christmas wreath.

There was even coffee brewing, compliments of First Sergeant, a Keurig he had gotten at the post PX for the rest of his Battery so their mornings would be somewhat normal. Someone had even dropped a small box of white, powdered donuts with Christmas sprinkles next to the coffee maker, the seal on it not broken yet.

That won't last long, Corporal Hicks knew, looking around at the famished admin around her. They got chow, yes, but delicacies like sweets, soda, and other heavy snacks were always at a minimum around the office, especially overseas. But last week, Christmas cookies were on the table, the weeks before, left overs from Thanksgiving, which required an extra table to be moved in temporarily to house all the food.

The holidays just do something to people, make them more softhearted or something, Hicks decided, straightening a stray blond hair that had come down from the bun she had put her hair in just a few minutes earlier. It was cleaned up around the neck, many of the stray hairs that had always littered her neck combed up or trimmed off so that her neckline was even and looked more like a soldiers and not just some woman in BDU's.

However, even with all of the Christmas items that the make-shift post was outfitted with, Justine couldn't get over the inevitable feeling of the Christmas Blues that creeped in ever so slowly. The 23-year-old woman missed her family, her friends, her hometown of Akron she had grown up in. She missed the several feet of snow that came down every year and going to get the tree with her father and two older brothers on Thanksgiving Day, just after the turkey and football ritual that they had perfected so well.

She didn't have time to reminisce much, though, for she heard someone approaching from behind.

And the morning starts here at the wonderful administration building!

"Specialist David Meyers, reporting for duty!" Meyers was always an over eager soldier. Justine could hear his boots click together, his form in attention always so tight and stiff.

It wasn't a bad position, just something not many took so serious while overseas, Justine thought, the many others loosening up around a great many new individuals over the last few months. But Meyers was still wet behind the ears. He had been attached to her Battery with the communications platoon, mainly because they said his platoon was the most efficient when it came to setting up and breaking down.

David was still standing at attention in front of her.

This was the administration office, not the quad or drill inspection!

"At ease, soldier!"

He dropped from attention to rest at ease, putting his hat into his cargo pouch at his knee. His hair was cut close to his head but Justine could see the start of growth beneath the thick sheen of gel on the top of his head.

"Morning, Meyers. You letting the top grow out?"

"Morning, Corporal. Really, you can tell already?" Meyers ran a hand over his slick-backed hair nervously, looking around the admin office.

"Chill, Meyers, I'm just kidding. It's fine. If you must know, it makes you look less green."

But he was still a bit nervous. "Is that a good thing or a bad thing?"

Justine smiled at him. He was cute, that was for sure, but in a very disarming, almost boyish way. Even though he had been here merely three months after finishing Basic and his A.I.T. training, he still very much looked the part of a scared kid on the first day of basic when they pulled everyone out of the cattle cars.

Crossing the tracks, Hicks recalled, the bumpy spot of train tracks that signaled that you were moving from reception battalion into basic training territory, where you would soon learn the meaning of the importance of breath mints. Hicks recalled a great many faces in her own those first few weeks, many of them in desperate need of a mint, a bottle of Listerine, *or a quick splash of bleach for some,* Hicks thought, remembering Drill Sergeant Tags quite well for his rancid breath.

Meyers was just another in the line of many coming in on rotation. Sometimes it was 6-months, other times it was a year or more. However long, Justine was always seeing new faces.

New deployments came in all the time for different reasons, Justine knew, having to process the paperwork for the soldiers when they came in.

"It's a good thing, Meyers. You don't want to look like you just walked out of basic straight into deployment."

He nodded his understanding. "Gotcha. Sounds reasonable."

"So, corporal, what do we have on the agenda for today?"

"Quite a bit, actually. We have some in-processing today, so we'll need to set up some more chairs in the waiting room, we need to file away the paperwork from yesterday," the corporal motioned over to the stack of papers in folders sitting on her desk not far away from the front desk where they stood now, "and we are tasked to help decorate the chow hall for the next few days since Christmas is almost upon us."

She didn't know what it was, but something she had said made his eyes glimmer more than they ever had before. It came and went quickly and he smiled and was soon back to his normal self.

"Wow, that's quite a bit. You want to break it up into pieces and we work on different things each? Or-"

She already knew what the second possibility was. Several times, Meyers had flirted with her, only to get the cold shoulder from her over and over again.

"We can start with the chow hall. Breakfast just wrapped and lunch won't be too far away. If we do the other work right now, we'll get caught in the lunch rush and won't be able to finish. Once we're done with that, I can finish filing the paperwork and you can get the spare chairs from the storage room and bring them and we can set them up in the waiting room.

"Sounds like a plan, corporal."

"You don't have to say that every time I ask for your help, Meyers. It gets annoying after a while."

"Well, you are my superior."

"Only by a few months. It was sheer luck I got promoted before you. You told me you were in line for promotion before you left and even have more time in than me."

"Two months, three days more, actually."

"So, please, for my Christmas present from you to me, can you just chill out on the formality?"

"I'll try, Hicks."

That was the first time he had called her by her last name. It felt refreshing to hear it instead of the proper title all the time.

"See, you're on your way to being a comfortable soldier among others!" Meyers nodded and flipped his hat onto his head, following behind the corporal as they made their way to the chow hall.

The exterior of the chow hall looked like all the other buildings that were on the post; the only exception was that there was a small smoke stack sitting on the top of the one-story building, a thick plume of smoke coming out from the kitchen section. Even though it wasn't anywhere near lunchtime yet, the line cooks were busy at work preparing lunch for hundreds of soldiers that would be coming through the door shortly.

Corporal Hicks and Specialist Meyers slipped into the side door of the chow hall, taking off their duty uniform caps as they entered. There were over a dozen line cooks away from the line at the moment, a flurry of activity in the kitchen as they mixed, stewed, added ingredients, and went to the freezer to get more things to prepare for the Christmas dinner.

And for the party, Christine reminded herself, the thoughts of the package she had received only days earlier coming to mind then. And it wasn't just any package, either; it was a package to get her freak on.

Let us get this out in the air real quick; the package wasn't sent to impress Specialist Meyers. There was no way that this was happening. There was another enlisted man stationed here that the attention was going to.

And, when Justine looked over at Meyers then, she knew why immediately. Meyers was still green. That and he looked as though he had never gotten laid. From the crisp duty uniform to the well-polished boots, it looked as though all Meyers thought about was his job and the time it took to get ready for it. But that didn't stop him from trying to get her to go out with him. And the responses went something like this every time.

'We work too close together,' or 'It would be like dating my little brother', Justine would say, but it would never quite click inside of Meyer's head. No matter how many times she said no, Specialist Meyers was one resilient soldier.

I had to at least give him credit for that, she thought to herself, finishing up the last of the decorations for the table dressing that the Christmas dinner would be placed on in a few minutes.

And in a few short hours, there will be a party like none other. Everyone will be there, and in fantastic fashion.

Chapter Two
- The Knock down -

Christine had never seen so much alcohol in all her life shared among friends. Of course, she was presently around rough-and-tumble soldiers, all wanting to de-stress from their present environment, wanting to see their family and, first and foremost, wanting to get laid.

Christine wasn't the only enlisted female there, which was a good thing for her. She had never seen so much man flesh bared in her life, (shown in the customary spirit of camaraderie, of course.) Bulging biceps, heaving, thickly muscled chests, fantastic abdominals flexing again and again repeatedly, as well as a few well-defined asses that spilled out of their duty uniforms now and then in rigorous party fashion of the season, keeping cool whilst the wintry season wore on all the way on the other side of the world.

This soldier wasn't easily swayed by an attractive physique but, seeing the large number of sweaty, well-muscled men in front of her dancing to Jingle Bell Rock on the portable speakers positioned at two corners of the room, it was hard not to fantasize about what could happen.

How would it go down, an orgy? Would one couple just start making out and others join in? Would it be like that? Or would there be undressing and touching first? Would the drink take someone over and a cockflash itself to everyone, an eager female soldier taking it up in her mouth to satiate the desires of herself and many others? Would there be a gangbang, doubling up on the female soldiers?

Justine knew a few women that wouldn't mind that at all, especially with all of the sexual tension going around this holiday season.

All these porn videos make it look so easy, she thought, checking out the thrusting hip movements of some of the other soldiers, knowing that anyone that got involved with them would be in for a thorough fucking. She had already heard from some of the other female soldiers how sex was with the male soldiers, a few of them taking several lovers over the past few months of being overseas.

But would everyone be nice and share if everyone were getting to fuck; or would there be those that were greedy and wanted another all to themselves? After all, we weren't in normal, societal conditions.

With being overseas so long and away from home and whatever normal looked like to everyone else, the rules and norms were changed; *bent was more the proper word.*

There were no snow-adorned homes positioned neatly in a row outside or chimneys keeping the loving family safe and warm. There was, however, a ragged tree dressed and decorated for Christmas in the corner of the rec room, presents lined around it in anticipation of Christmas morning, which was rapidly approaching.

And then there was the man she was waiting for; Sergeant Ryan Breckenridge. If ever there was a specimen of a man that Christine would let writhe on top of her in pleasure and shake his extremities in post-coital pleasure, it was this man. Christine and a great many other female soldiers had taken a liking to his presence and form immediately after they arrived on post, watching as he took his rank and position seriously, but played and enjoyed himself just a seriously when it was down time. It was as if there were two different versions of him, just waiting for a woman to offer themselves to him. And offer they did.

But he had a thing for her only; for poor little Justine Hicks, a girl from nowhere who knew nobody, but wanted more than anything to know this man. And in the biblical sense as well. The kitty between her legs easily became a wellspring whenever they talked or got close to one another. And, many times, she had no idea how he didn't act on this closeness, as if he were the master of his own emotions and hers as well.

That's why Justine had to have a little bit of the liquid courage to get her going. She had never dealt with a man of this caliber before; tall, handsome, good-looking in every way, shape and form. She took a few shots with the girls to start, then another shot or two with her admin crew to finish off. By the last shot, her body was warm and ready for anything that the hunky soldier had to throw at her.

We won't have to wait much longer, Justine reminded herself, moving away from the crowd of soldiers then, taking a drink with her outside of the rec room. And, with the music being so loud and as so many people were piled into one area, no one took notice of her being gone.

Justine was able to slip away to her and Ryan's planned meeting place; one of the offices in the admin building. They couldn't exactly go get a hotel or go back to their own barracks with knowing others would soon arrive. They were both doing their best to be as discreet as possible. With her leaving first, she would be able to get out the package and prep for his arrival.

The package had been sent by one of her more willing friends back home. She had asked for some sexy lingerie to get freaky in, gave her friend her measurements, and wasn't disappointed at all when she received the package a few weeks later, just in time for tonight. First of all, it was incredibly festive. The corset was black with little red bows adorning it down the middle, just between her ample bosom, one bow a little larger than the others sewn in just at the edge where her cleavage met together. The matching panties were a simple black lace but crotchless, something Justine had never tried before but was definitely willing to with Sergeant Sexy Pants. There was also a pair of black stockings with small print designs on them, both which she slipped on now.

Along with an ample supply of condoms and lube and a vibrator thrown in the package by her friend for shits and giggles and a card that read, 'Merry Fucking Christmas' with the 'Fucking' underlined multiple times, Justine was as prepared as she was ever going to be.

Justine was about to know how it felt to be naughty. Back home in the states, she had been a rather good girl, taking her time to get to know the men around her way before she got involved with any of them. Sure, the twenty-three year old had done some kinky sex positions with her last ex-boyfriend, even going into a little foreplay for him with some slight dress-up, showing off her tight curves. But nothing like this; nothing so informal.

She looked at herself now, all decked out in her sexy attire, primed and at the ready for a man she barely knew, waiting to have hot, dirty sex with him on the floor on some blankets and pillows. She smiled and smacked her ass in excitement.

Justine's ass had always been firm and rather plump, jutting out enough to catch the attention of most guys in high school and her first two years of college before joining the military.

Now, her ass was the epitome of perfect.

After Basic Training, Justine had kept a serious workout regimen on her legs, thighs, and ass. Her lower extremities were rather exposed now with just the right amount of black, Christmas lace adorning them. As for her breasts, they were nothing to scoff at either. She didn't need a push-up bra to get ample enough cleavage to attract attention and they were firm enough to keep close to her body when she ran p.t. in the mornings. Many a boyfriend spent a great deal of time under her shirt, so she didn't feel as though there would be any complaints from the present party about to come in through the personnel door in the back.

And, for the main event, Justine felt down between her legs once again and felt nothing but smoothness below.

He keeps talking that shit about what he can do with that mouth, she reminded herself, pressing her middle finger into her moistness, her entire body waiting in anticipation of the naughtiness to come.

Alright, you better get your Robin Thicke look alike, built-ass over here before I start without you, Breckenridge!

Justine could feel herself becoming light-headed from the rush of blood moving down to her nether regions. She licked her lips at the thought of the Sergeant diving into her freshly-shaven kitten ever so properly. She slowly crossed her legs over one another to stop her fingers from continuing and slipped her finger free from her throbbing foxhole.

Just then, she heard the doorknob shake and her body shook with excitement in response, her nipples pressing out against the sheer fabric of the Christmas lingerie.

Has he arrived, asked her perk nipples, nearly cutting through the silkiness in excitement.

Yes, he has, her quivering knees answered in response, moving over to the pallet she had made for them on the floor, sliding herself down onto the soft pile of blankets to wait for him. She remembered that he had said that he had a surprise for her and, as the door opened, she suddenly knew what it was.

A fully dressed Santa Claus stood at the doorway, looking down at her half-naked form on the floor. She was nearly bursting with anticipation at having him all over her and having some alone time after being cooped up at that party and planning for it for days on end.

"Well, if it isn't Santa Claus, come to deliver presents on Christmas Eve."

He let out an uproarious, "Ho, Ho, Ho!" just as if he were the real Santa Claus, covering his belly with a hand and laughing merrily as he closed the door behind him with the other.

It took Justine all the courage that she had to pull off naughty, but she went for broke and spoke again, lifting up the lace lingerie to show off her dainty, crotchless panties that she had gotten just for him. She shook with delight at his arrival, wiggling her ass on the soft blankets underneath her.

"Now, if I'm correct, Santa has some cookies to eat before he can leave, isn't that right?"

The fully bearded Santa nodded his jolly head and proceeded to get down on all fours, crawling over to her. His thick, fake beard nearly dragged on the ground, his Santa hat falling forward a little bit as he positioned himself between her legs.

"You must be hungry after your long trip here." Justine ushered his beard in between her legs and felt the pleasure surge through her as Santa's tongue dove into her warm and inviting chimney.

"Oooooh, that feels so good, Santa! Yeah, right there!"

Justine put her hands atop Santa's head to direct him, holding his face down against the warm fireplace between her legs. Santa continued, with directions, Justine forcing his tongue onto her clit, receiving each tongue lash of pleasure he was giving with a squeak or moan escaping her lips.

"Oh my goodness! Eat those cookies, Santa! That feels-that feels so fucki-"

The words caught in her throat as she came, Santa's beard rubbing against the inside of her legs, tickling and turning her on at the same time. She had never come that quickly before.

Maybe it was just the anticipation building. Maybe it was my fingers playing that started it all. Or maybe- maybe this man was on his game.

Whatever the case, she didn't want to ruin the moment and overanalyze it, let alone forget about the pleasure that was pulsing through her right now, causing her toes to curl.

Justine stopped trying to control Santa with her hands and felt Santa's gloved hands then gripping her legs. She looked down between her thighs, her eyes glazed over from the pleasure.

He spoke in his silly Santa voice again, his breath heavy against the inside of her legs.

"That's a good girl. And some good cookies. I think I'll take seconds, if you don't mind. It's gotten me rather... hungry."

And, again, Santa's head began to move with the strokes of his tongue, sometimes fast and hard, a few times slow and steady. The entire time this time, his gloved hands were holding her thighs steady, keeping Justine from moving or wiggling. She could do nothing but accept eagerly the eating of her cookies again, even though her chimney was on fire from the last explosion below. Her toes were throbbing in pleasure, her thighs were shaking with delight, she knew she would be pleased with what Santa brought her this year.

"Oh, fuck Santa! Fuck you, Santa! That feels so fucking good! I'm coming again!" She was out of breath now, this time feeling the surge between her legs become uncontrollable. As her orgasm pulsed through her, she looked up from her position, grabbing at the Santa hand to hold the jolly old elf steady as her pleasured waned. That's when the hat came off with the white Santa hair, revealing not Sergeant Breckenridge as she had thought, but a young, eager-to-please Specialist Meyers covered in her juices.

And it was then that Corporal Justine Hicks felt the full effect of the orgasm take effect, the blood rushing back to her head so suddenly that she passed out with Santa having properly finished up his cookie eating between her legs.

*   *   *

Justine didn't know what time it was when she awoke, but it was still not yet morning, for the sun wasn't coming through the windows of the administrative office. She was half-awake and noticed that she was alone on the mass of blankets by the office, the door closed tightly from whence Santa Claus had come.

"Where did he go? What happened after he ate my cookies?" She looked around for any signs of sex play afterword and found none, though her chimney was still warm and slick with her own orgasms. That's when she heard the doorknob wiggle and then open, Justine covering up in one of the blankets underneath her.

Please don't be First Sergeant! My world will be over from here on out and I'll never live this moment down!

But it wasn't him. She was glad for that. However, it was the weirdest thing. Stumbling across the room after barely being able to close the door, was a drunken Sergeant Ryan Breckenridge, doing his best to be the Santa Claus that they had planned together, half-holding a bottle of Jack Daniels loosely.

"Ho, ho, ho," was his best drunk Santa bit, slurring his speech. It took a moment but he looked down and saw Corporal Hicks on the floor in her lingerie and tried his best to get down on all fours and crawl. He tumbled, almost headfirst, to the floor.

"Sorry I'm late, baby. The guys kept the party going and wouldn't let me leave." In another 30 seconds, he was passed out and snoring by her feet.

Wouldn't let you leave, Justine questioned, looking down at the Santa suit. It looked nothing like the suit that had come in earlier. This one was some cheap knock-off suit that you could buy at any store. But the other one, it was much more-elaborate. In fact, Justine remembered now not being able to see the person's face at all until the last moment. All she felt was the trusty tongue beneath the white beard, lolling and lapping, lapping and flicking, pressing and pushing.

There was no mistaking Specialist Meyers between her legs earlier and the urgency that she had made him go down on her. Even with the suit on, how could she be fooled? She hadn't had too much to drink. She was his superior. How was this going to look in the morning.

All she knew is that she was swimming in pleasure at the moment and Breckenridge was in no shape to eat any cookies or go riding on a sleigh.

CHAPTER THREE
- TASTE OF THE YUMMY -

"What the hell happened to you last night, Sergeant?" She looked over at Breckenridge that morning at chow, setting her tray down directly across from him. She sat down in front of him.

No longer did the Sergeant look like Robin Thicke. He looked like a hammered, beaten, and drugged version of an older Robin Thicke. He tried his best to smile but it did him no good. Breckenridge looked in pain when he tried grabbing for the orange juice on his tray.

"I celebrated way too hard with the platoon, Corporal. The only thing I remember is waking up outside next to the latrine covered in my own piss. I guess you're mad at me now, huh?"

Now this part was somewhat difficult for Justine.

Do I tell him about the cookie-eating of my life by another man and of him passing out in the midst of trying to score with me or do I just let it go?

"I'm not mad, you just missed out on a good night, Sergeant. I heard Santa Claus came last night. What did he give you?"

Breckenridge finished the last of his orange juice and took a few breaths before answering.

"A fucking hangover, that's what he gave me. And short-term memory loss."

Maybe it wasn't a good idea to say anything yet, Justine thought, trying her best to figure out how to go about this situation.

She got up from her seat in front of Breckenridge after a few bites, leaving her food right where it was.

"Hey, Corporal, where are you going?" She didn't respond. By the time she thought about what to say to the Sergeant, she was already out the door and on her way, crossing the quad to the men's barracks. Once she got there, she walked in and looked around for Specialist Meyers. He wasn't there, but there were others. She called on them for answers.

"Where's Meyers?"

One of the privates pointed over to Meyers' bunk and then to his laundry bag and towel.

"It's his day off so he usually gets a shower and goes to do his wash." Christine nodded and continued on her way to the laundry facility, a separate area from the living quarters completely.

Justine looked at the laundry facility but he wasn't there.

Must be at the showers then. Justine knew that this would probably be the only time to catch him before she had to report for duty at the personnel office after chow.

The showers were made to house at least 14 people at a time, using a large drum of water that gets heated to a warm enough temperature that has pipes that run to 14 different spouts that can adjust the temperature. There's a concrete base built with five-foot high walls to keep the sand and dust out of the shower area. There were two entrances, one on the north side and one on the south. Justine took the south entrance and walked in. There was only one shower going at this time of the day and Specialist Meyers was occupying it.

Being in the military kept her from being shy around others that were naked. It wasn't something to be ashamed of. But, for some reason, Justine thought about what happened last night and, if Meyers was the culprit, it would make it difficult to be around him.

"Meyers!" Meyers turned around when he heard the corporal's voice, still covered in suds but otherwise in the buff. He still looked very much like a young man just blossoming into manhood. He had very little hair on his body at all, with the exception of the small goody trail that went down to his pubic hair. There was little hair on his legs but they were tanned and muscular for a man of such small stature.

And the glimpse Justine got of the specialist's privates was enough to know that he could take care of things in the fucking department.

He didn't look surprised to see her.

"Good morning, Corporal. Merry Christmas."

Corporal Hicks had totally forgotten that it was Christmas Day. In the passing of such a great night, she had a great many other things on her mind.

"You mind telling me where you were at 2300 last night?" Whatever toughness she had she used now, her voice stronger than it had ever been before.

"Am I being questioned for something, Corporal?" And there was something in his smile, something different than she could see that hadn't been there before.

"I just need to know, Meyers."

"Well, I was with you last night, Corporal. Don't you remember? You shoved me between your legs before I could say anything."

Well, if that just isn't fucking great! A new soldier arrives to the battalion and I end up putting him to work on my clit. That's going to look great on any report.

"I had a little too much to drink, I think."

"So, you don't remember me climbing down between your legs and-"

"Yes! Yes, Meyers! That part I do remember. You want to tell me how you knew I was going to be there?"

He rinsed his hair before answering, taking his time, getting every little bit of suds off his head, the water trailing to parts unknown that Justine had yet to see. She tried to keep her bearings on the questions at hand.

"I didn't know. I noticed you had left as was just checking to make sure you were okay."

"So, you just happened to walk in and see me in a provocative state and make your move?"

"You asked me to. I was just playing the part of Santa. So I made a move."

"Your move being?"

"A rather strong one. I really didn't know what would happen when I went into the personnel office last night. I thought you'd spot that it was me before anything happened. When you didn't, I let the moment continue."

"You tasted my pussy, Meyers!" Justine was stuck between being in a blinding rage and being turned on at the fact that Meyers was capable of such an act.

"And it was delicious, Corporal. You were amazing last night."

"That's not why I'm here, Meyers!"

"Then why are you here, Corporal? Are you here to bust me out and get me a court martial for fraternizing with another soldier?"

"I'm not here for that either, Meyers. I wanted it just as much as you did. You just…you just.. don't understand! It was supposed to be my night last night!"

"Oh, it most definitely was, Corporal. There's no doubt there. It's easy how I see it. I've liked you since I arrived here and they put me under your jurisdiction. But you never gave me the time of day. Now I understand why. You like someone else. I get it."

"I don't. It's not like that!" There was no way to word it easily; she enjoyed Meyers between her legs. She knew it was him the whole time. She knew because she had bought Breckenridge the Santa suit. She knew it wasn't the same suit as soon as Meyers walked in.

Meyers continued. "I wasn't trying to take advantage of you! I just wanted to show you how much I liked you. And I just wanted you to trust me."

Meyers had finished his shower and was now just standing there in front of Christine in the buff. The water was dripping off of his form and apparently the conversation had struck a nerve with him because his member was now becoming rigid. Christine couldn't help but look. After last night, her insides were still throbbing from the pleasure.

"So, you didn't like what I did last night then, did you?"

"No, it's not that! I thought it was fantastic!" She did her best to downplay it. "I mean, it was good. I mean…it felt good."

"Well then, I have one question."

And, while saying that, Meyers pulled out a long, slender candy-cane shaped vibrator from his laundry bag that hung not far from him, switching it on. He pointed it at her, all the while his member getting harder in front of her. "Has Justine been good this Christmas?"

What could I have possibly done right to deserve this? Justine reached out to Meyers and took hold of him by the head then, kissing him hard on the lips.

Fuck it, I'm keeping him! Fuck messing with Breckenridge! It's not every day that you find a Santa that can eat your cookies as good as Meyers had done.

Corporal Hicks felt her inhibitions disappear and began taking off her p.t. uniform, soon being pulled into the searing hot water with Meyers, the tip of the candy cane shaped vibrator disappearing inside of her as the Specialist pulled her closer to him. He whispered in her ear.

"There's something about the holidays that just puts me in the mood, don't you agree?"

But Corporal Justine Hicks was too far in the throes of passion to respond, the vibration of the festive candy cane doing its job, keeping her on her toes until the throbbing took over and she was awash in pleasure.

And the answer to the young man's question?

Yes. Yes, Justine had been a good girl for Santa. And her Santa rewarded her with a lovely candy cane, time and again, until visions of sugarplums, among other things, danced in her head.

And, soon, she too began to have a thing for the holidays.

The End

AUTHOR'S NOTES

I envisioned this collection back in August of 2011, coming back from a great time in Chicago as part of my book tour for the first book in my erotic fiction series entitled The Temptress. I have a tendency to think a whole lot while driving (that total trip was 6990 miles, btw) and I had a notepad with me in the passenger's seat if I had ideas along the way.

I got the idea so quick that I called my graphic artist and told her the idea. In less than a month, the cover had been created for the book and the synopsis had been created for each story. However, for some reason, this book lay waiting inside my head for years. I let it sit there without ever really working on it. I worked on several other projects and got degrees, moved around a bit, did some slave labor at my job, you know, the normal daily grind.

But, when I sat down with this series of short stories, I always had a hard time with the characters. 'How am I going to give all of these characters justice and hope for the holidays,' I said to myself, 'all the while giving my readers the perversion that they deserve?' I wanted each character, each story, each wet, dripping moment to be better than the last, but I didn't want to make the stories so outlandish that they couldn't be real scenes in someone's life as well.

I noticed that, as I got older (and wiser and sexier, of course), I saw the steps that each of these characters took towards their own goals. Even if they were only short-term goals, they had wants, needs, and desires just like the rest of us here on Planet Earth. As I pounded away at the keys (and other things), I made sure that there was plenty of depravity and naughtiness, especially in time for Christmas. I had always wanted to finish this novel before Christmas but, when I sat down at the old keys of wisdom, nothing came out. It wasn't that I wasn't inspired, lost the holiday spirit or had writer's block. In fact, I loved every story, every character, even the ones that weren't too good to begin with.

This novel may have taken me the longest to complete in a while, but the spirit of the holidays is in there, within every story, within every depraved page, just waiting to get out and wreak havoc on your calm holidays. I'm proud to give you the first of many; a festive collection of short stories that are sure to have you stuffing someone's stocking.

Happy Holidays,
my merry mischief-makers.

About the Author

Little is known about the author TITUS STRONG. Taking his name from a classic Shakespearean dramatic protagonist, Titus Andronicus, the author writes stories that fill the imagination with lust and humor, all the while waiting for his own next sexual conquest, forever filling his time with fantasies that wait to be fulfilled themselves.

OTHER BOOKS BY TITUS STRONG:

<u>A Man's Romance Novel Series:</u>

- **Book 1: The Temptress: (Released 08/2011)**
- A Corporate Feeling: Book Two (TBA)
- Teach Me: Book Three (TBA)
- Domesticating the Inner Hound: Book Four (TBA)
- **How Santa Ate My Cookies and Other Festive Tales of Erotic Fiction (Released 12/2018)**

<u>A Young Gentleman's Romance Novel Series:</u>

- **The Pill: Book One (Released 10/2014)**
- The Pill: Second Dose (TBA)
- The Pill: Possible Solutions (TBA)

Now you can order your
Exclusive Books and Merchandise from
Wunderlannd Press Publishing directly!

GO TO: mkt.com/wunderlanndpress **or** use the QR Code below with your tablet or mobile device for great goodies only available on the company store. You can even get limited copies autographed and personalized by select authors free of charge.

Also available for purchase at these local retailer sites:

www.amazon.com and www.bandn.com, www.alibris.com